DANGEROUS DETOUR

Gail Pallotta

Dedication – To Carolyn, Gary, Linda and Sue

Acknowledgements – The cover photo is "Courtesy of Western Carolina University" in Cullowhee, North Carolina. Many thanks to the college for the picture and to Jayson Litrio for enhancing the photo. I'm grateful to Deputy Sheriff Jon Teusink for his input and to my family and friends who support my writing. I thank Cynthia Hickey for giving me the opportunity to share *Dangerous Detour*. I thank the Lord for giving me the words to write and opening the doors along the way to publication.

Chapter One

Twilight fell.

The fog grew thicker, and ice pellets hit the windshield.

Ruthie O'Donnell wished she'd waited to leave for home tomorrow, but the weatherman had forecast snow, not ice.

Her car skidded.

A drop-off on the right. An embankment on the left.

Holding the steering wheel so tight her knuckles hurt, Ruthie turned the wheel with the slide. Thud. The airbag deployed. Her horn honked.

The motor ground into the quiet night. After the airbag deflated, with her hand shaking, she turned off the engine, opened the door, and stepped out. The beams from the car's headlights shone on the hood.

She'd smashed into a tall oak growing on the side of a cliff. Only the tree kept her from tumbling over the steep precipice. When her knees went weak, she braced herself on the doorframe, slid into the driver's seat, and collapsed on the airless airbag.

Metal grinding against metal blasted, then the world fell silent. Ruthie stared at the soft snow. She could almost hear the mist.

Tapping. From far away? Someone coming to help? Or hurt her? Every muscle in her body tightened.

"Ma'am, Ma'am, are you alright?"

A large man holding a flashlight stood by the car.

She started closing the door, but he pulled it open. She scrunched her shoulders and recoiled.

Placing a muscular arm around her waist, the man gently pulled her out as though she weighed no more than a light grocery bag. After he stood her up on the highway, she stiffened at his size. Towering over her five-feet-four inches, he had broad shoulders, dark hair, and…wait. Did kindness glint in his big brown eyes, or did she imagine it?

"Ma'am, we need to get your belongings out in case your vehicle goes over."

Ruthie looked at her car and placed her hand over her mouth.

"Ma'am, I didn't mean to upset you more than this disaster already has." He sighed. "Before I left, I listened to a weather forecast for the Western North Carolina Mountains for snow, possibly heavy at times."

"I heard snow too."

"We're lucky. I skidded into the guardrail sideways and stopped ten feet behind you. We came so close…" The man motioned toward the bluff. "But here we are." He peeked in the backseat window. "We need to take only the most important things—suitcase, water, food. Any of that buried under all of those books?"

Trying to assess her situation, Ruthie pondered the words before she answered. "I have luggage in the trunk and one to-go box of food."

"I'll grab your bag if you'll bring the leftovers."

"What about my car?"

"The tree holding it appears pretty sturdy. Strong winds, ice and hail could damage it though. Considering the conditions and the one-hundred-foot drop, I wouldn't try to move it. If it slides sideways, it could plummet over the edge." He glanced at her backseat again. "Could you choose a few of those books and leave the rest?"

She held the duffle bag in one hand and the food in the other. "That's all right. I don't have to take them." She valued her books like gold nuggets, but she could only carry so much. When the man had said one-hundred-foot drop, she had put her desire to read in perspective.

"I know how bookworms are about their pastime. Take a few. I'll add your items to mine and carry them all."

Wait a minute. Twilight had turned to night, and here she was, standing on the side of the highway in a storm talking to a strange man as big as Paul Bunyon? "Who are you?"

"Should've introduced myself right away. I only considered our situation and how we must get to a safe place. Moose, I'm Moose Byer."

"I'm Ruthie O'Donnell." Ruthie flicked snowflakes off of her nose. Then, she studied the man through a veil of tiny white, irregular shapes. She could see why someone called him Moose, but surely his parents didn't.

"Uh, I'm Moose to my friends, but my given name is George."

Did the concern ringing in his voice mean he was a caring person? Did she really need him to rescue her? She gave her car a second look. Maybe she could turn on the heater and sleep in the backseat. She could at least sit in the front and wait for help.

No. In the end, it came down to the car stuck there waiting for a stiff breeze to push it over the cliff. If it fell, she would not want to go with it. If she couldn't stay in the car, what would she do out here by herself? As if nature intended to sway her decision, a strong gust of icy wind slapped her in the face. "I see. I can't move my car, and even if I could, the road's not suitable for travel."

"That's right, ma'am. We need to get out of the snow and bitter temperature. I'm bringing my personal bag and football gear. It consists of first aid supplies, extra pants, shirts, most everything we need."

What was he talking about? She knew exactly what to do. "Have you called the police?"

Moose sighed. "There's no signal."

Ruthie pulled her cell phone out of her purse and checked it. Moose was right. "What do you propose?" she asked.

"If you don't want to freeze, we have to find shelter. From my hunting days with my dad, I know of a deserted cabin."

Ruthie's pulse beat in her temples. She couldn't go traipsing through the forest with a total stranger. What if he dragged her into the cabin and raped or killed her? She let her eyes meet his, but they told her nothing, except he didn't blink. What did that mean? He checked his watch, which probably meant he wanted to leave.

"There's nowhere to stay on the highway, least of

all in our cars with the wind whipping around them. I promise I'll take care of you."

How could she think straight looking at her car threatening to topple over a cliff and the storm blowing around her? She couldn't, but she saw one thing clearly—she didn't get to choose. She needed leverage though. She pressed her lips tight. "I'd rather not wander too far. I imagine someone will see this disaster at daybreak and start looking for us." There. She had planted a seed letting the big man know he better not harm her, hadn't she?

"Under normal circumstances that's exactly what would happen, but we barely missed a huge rockslide."

Ruthie put her hands over her ears, nearly dropping the leftovers. Enough. "Are we trapped?" Even in the thick mist she could see her frenzied breath.

Moose scrubbed his hand over his face. "Not exactly. The road leading to Misty Ridge, a little farther south is clear of debris, but it's closed."

"Why?"

"Obviously, you don't live around here."

"I'm originally from the Florida Panhandle. I moved to Western North Carolina this fall."

Moose shifted his weight. "We're a victim of cold air damming."

"I've never heard of such a thing."

"Well, you wouldn't in Florida. In short, cold air presses against the mountains and stays there instead of moving to the other side as usual. When warm air blows in, the two meet, and we have this."

"I see."

"The roads can freeze then refreeze as soon as DOT cleans them. The authorities have no choice, but to close them. We need to go now. Put a few books in your bag, and I'll take it."

Ruthie did as he asked. Then, he stuffed it inside his larger gear and pulled out two thermos bottles. "Coffee leftover from breakfast." He shot Ruthie a face-splitting grin as though he was proud of his offering. "One's mine, but a friend asked me to hold onto his drink for a minute then he hopped in his car and drove off without it." He winked at Ruthie. "It's yours."

He held them out to her and she took them. "If you can carry those and your to-go box, I'll take everything else. At least we can rest out of the elements."

Ruthie placed her purse in the crook of her arm and hooked the handles on the thermos bottles on her wrist. She couldn't survive outdoors or sleep in her car. No one would show up to rescue her. The muscle in her cheek twitched at what she was about to do.

Moose got the flashlight out of his bag then put one bag over his left shoulder and grasped the other in his left hand, carrying them with no effort.

Two steps and Ruthie slipped.

Moose steadied her before she hit the icy pavement.

Soon they reached the edge of the woods. Her muscles tightened as she crunched into the hoary wilderness on slippery terrain. The flashlight shone barely twenty feet on their path. They plodded over sticks, pebbles, and leaves, all covered in winter's blanket. The trees with icicles over their bare branches resembled ghosts.

Ruthie wore the down coat and leather gloves Mom gave her before she moved. Still, winter's biting temperature chilled her to the bone. She tripped again. Moose took hold of her, kept her from falling. She wasn't cut out for the great outdoors in the summer let alone in this storm. She looked up at Moose. "Thank you."

"You're welcome." He spoke in a matter-of-fact tone.

She appreciated not going ka-splat on the frigid ground. Still, his support hadn't made her more comfortable around him. Did he have an ulterior motive for their arrival at the cabin? Worse yet, was there a cabin? Walking farther into the forest with him, the snow and wind biting her cheeks, she wasn't sure which she feared most—Moose or the elements.

The light bounced off her shoes and Moose said, "Decorative tennis shoes aren't fit for this weather."

"I wasn't planning on schlepping through a glacial forest."

"It's okay. We'll make it. It can't be much farther."

Moose's words sounded as though someone sucked the confidence out of them. An afternoon snack Ruthie ate swished in her stomach, crawled up her throat, and gagged her. She swallowed hard to keep from throwing up, but an upchucking noise erupted.

Moose stopped in his tracks. "Are you alright?"

"Of course, I'm fine." She wouldn't dare let him know she was scared to death of him. Maybe if she started a conversation, she would get to know him better. "When do you think we'll get phone service?"

Moose studied their path before he started walking again. "Hard to say."

Why didn't he want to talk? "How much farther to the cabin?"

"Hard to say."

"Don't you ever say anything other than hard to say?"

Moose pulled a slow grin. "Sometimes, maybe later."

Finally, she'd changed his staid expression, but one smile didn't tell her much about him. She gave up on finding out anything about him anytime soon. Nothing stirred in the forest as though the animals had all run for shelter, or frozen to death. The silence of the cold, black night, made her quiver. Moose was right about one thing.

The cabin was a good idea. They could build a fire and eat. That was it. There was no ulterior motive. Her nerves had spun out of control creating suspicion and making her overly sensitive—she hoped. She placed her hand on her tummy. She wasn't sure she could eat.

Even if Moose treated her with kindness and acted like a perfect gentleman, the wild animals posed a threat. Everything from cougars to raccoons and possums roamed these mountains. Her blood ran cold, but there were birds too. Yes, birds. The Bible said if God took care of the birds, He'd take care of her.

Still, going deeper into the dark forest required all of the fortitude she could muster. When would she see the cabin?

Chapter Two

"Do the right thing because it's the right thing to do." Moose recalled the words his mom ingrained in him. If he hadn't gotten out of his wrecked vehicle to investigate the screeching sound of metal piercing the night, it would've haunted him for the rest of his life.

When he put himself in Ruthie's situation, he understood her hesitancy to go into the woods with a stranger. The cabin was her and his best hope of not freezing though. He glanced at her. How much more problematic could the difficulties created by this storm get?

Poor lady, he'd do his best to keep her from falling to pieces until the temperature rose above freezing and DOT cleaned the road. He couldn't imagine why anyone would want to talk in the middle of a storm, but apparently this woman did.

She probably needed to hear something pleasant, especially about these woods. "It seems odd walking through here without listening to the squirrels break twigs while they're playing. It's just too chilly for them. They'll probably come out tomorrow when the weather warms up. Don't get me wrong, it won't thaw."

Satisfied he'd made his point he tried to sound friendly. "Do you like to watch the squirrels?"

She grinned so big her cheeks probably hurt from the effort in this frigid air. Yeah, he needed to talk along with everything else he did to keep them safe.

"I haven't made squirrel watching a pastime, but I could try it."

"I guess you haven't had time with your nose in all those books."

Ruthie flashed angry green eyes at him. "I'll beg your pardon."

Even after he chose his words carefully, he'd inadvertently sparked her hot wire. What an aggravation. "I didn't mean to offend you, ma'am. It's obvious you spend lots of time reading." Finally, he spotted a boulder he remembered and shined the flashlight on it. "We're nearly there. See that big rock?"

When she looked in the direction he pointed, her long, strawberry blonde curls bounced around her green toboggan, which matched her clear, green eyes. Seeing the innocence in them, he was glad he had heeded his mother's words. This woman needed his help.

"Do you recognize it?"

"Sure do. I've looked for it all the way. It's close to the cabin. Ah, there it is." He focused the light on a log structure. "Just as I remember it when I came with Dad on our hunting trip."

Ruthie lifted her brows. "What if it's locked?"

"I don't recall a lock, but we can always break in if we have to." Moose spoke with a stern voice to prepare her for their accommodations before they went inside. "It's dirty and not in good shape. You know, rickety walls, that sort of thing, but there's a big fireplace. It shouldn't take long to get a blaze going. It might seem a bit backwoods for your taste."

"No, I mean, yes, you're right. I only stay where I can plug in my hair dryer. Tonight, this cabin looks like a palace though. I understand. It's much better than sleeping outside."

~

After the walk through the wilderness with snowflakes hitting Ruthie's nose, she appreciated Mom and Dad's love of Florida more than ever. She wished she had landed a job there. So far, she had enjoyed her work as an advanced grammar professor at Hilltop College. She had liked the North Carolina Mountains fine—until today.

"Come on."

"Okay." She started walking again, this time without hesitation. Had something about Moose's nature broken through to her? Or was it divine intervention letting her know she'd met a kind, caring person? Of course, she only had two choices—trust him or don't. She chose number one, at least for now.

"Shelter at last." Moose set down the luggage on a rickety plank porch. Then took a wide stance with his hands on his hips.

A strong presence hovered over Ruthie. No wonder he conquered the elements and brought her here safely. She put down the to-go box and thermoses and touched a narrow opening between two logs. "I guess the air blows through here?"

"It might, but it's colder outside." He swung open the door. "This thing's not insulated as we know it. Years ago, people around here stuffed the gaps with everything from their underwear to grass or mud." He motioned inside. "Your castle awaits."

Ruthie giggled partly at his joke, but mostly from relief there was a cabin. Grateful a strong wind no longer blew around her, she said, "Thank you."

"You're welcome." Moose locked a grin fit for a toothpaste commercial.

Ruthie strode farther into a large room with a table, sofa, and easy chair in front of a fireplace on the end wall. The sink and cabinets were to the left of the fireplace three feet from a tall window that resembled half of a French door. After a musty smell mixed with the odor of ashes accosted her nostrils, she scrutinized the area like a surveillance camera. "Uh, oh. It appears someone lives here."

Moose's eyes snapped wide. "What?"

Ruthie tried not to fidget, but her nerves crawled inside her like ants. "There's a dim light over the kitchen sink."

Moose looked around. "You're right. I was so glad we arrived safely I didn't pay enough attention to the place. It's old and out of the way, I just assumed…"

"I see why you thought no one lived here. It's dilapidated. The fireplace bothers me most though. The embers aren't smoldering, but the ashes appear recent."

"Maybe the people who live here are kind and will let us spend the night."

Clearly, Moose didn't know what she knew. What if the person here were…Surely not. Moose was probably right. More than likely, a good-hearted mountaineer had taken up residence in the cabin since Moose and his dad saw it. Still, he needed to know. "I heard a news alert on the car radio, saying a suspect who killed three people in a jewelry store robbery had fled to the North Carolina Mountains." She couldn't keep her voice from trailing off. "Uh, Damian Hucklesford. You don't think…"

"We need to go." Moose snatched the bags.

Ruthie grabbed the thermoses and leftover food. "Where?"

"I'm not sure." Moose hoisted one bag on his shoulder, held the other in his hand, and charged to the door. "I can barely see through the snow, but I think…yes, there's a man carrying a rifle and a sack of sticks walking this way."

"We can escape here."

"Where?"

Ruthie pointed to the window that looked like half of a French door. "We can stand up and walk through." She eyed him. "Will you fit?"

"I'll have to. Throw out the thermoses. Follow them as fast as you can."

Ruthie pushed on the casement. It swung open. Whew! She charged outside. Moose pitched out the bags.

Footfalls pounded the porch. Ruthie's throat turned as dry as a dessert.

Moose sucked in air, pushed hard, moved halfway, and his broad shoulders got stuck. He lunged forward. Nothing.

"Hurry." Ruthie yanked on his arm.

The steps grew closer.

Ruthie tugged on his waist.

He strained, grunted.

Branches hit the porch.

He pulled in his shoulders, grabbed the top jamb, and pushed. Ruthie pulled.

Footfalls pounded inside.

Ruthie yanked on Moose's belt. He pushed again. Finally, he fell out, facedown.

Footfalls headed toward the window.

Moose and Ruthie grabbed their bags.

Slipping, sliding, they raced into the woods.

Ruthie clutched Moose's arm. She had to keep up.

He stumbled.

Ruthie tripped.

After he steadied them, they jogged into white nothingness, Ruthie running two strides to his one.

Shots thundered in the distance.

Moose sped up. They skated farther into iced-over timberland.

Bang. Bang.

Bang.

Moose ran faster.

Ruthie panted.

Baaannng…

Ruthie barely heard the shot.

Moose stopped. "Either we've put enough distance between us, or he's taken a different route." Inhaling, exhaling in bursts, he dropped the bags and bent over.

Ruthie thanked the Lord for carrying her when she could not have kept up, and for leading them away from Hucklesford, at least for now. She'd never run so hard so fast in her entire life, especially on a surface that invited her to fall. She let go of the thermoses, set down the leftover food, and gasped for air. "Th-the ra-radio announcer said the murderer had a trim build, a beard, and long black hair. He was last seen wearing a motorcycle jacket and black pants. I don't know whether the man at the cabin was him or not."

Moose stood up straight. "It doesn't matter. Whoever he is, he shot at us."

Ruthie heard another bang in the distance. She removed her glove and wiped beads of sweat off of her upper lip. "Didn't we lose him? It's so slippery we can't go any faster. What are we going to do? He's going to kill us."

"Don't worry. He probably shot an animal." Uncertainty rang in Moose's voice.

"An animal.? Are you kidding? If that's so, the poor thing wasn't far behind us." Ruthie glimpsed the front of her coat as she bent down to pick up the food and thermoses. "Oh no, I'm missing a button. He's going to find it." Guilt washed over her like the low hanging fog. Even though she ran track in high school and broke a record, the blood of an English teacher ran through her. She existed in an erudite world. What did she know about criminals, let alone fleeing from one?

Moose waved his hand in the air. "Don't worry. Who would notice a little button?"

Ruthie pulled the front of the coat away from her body, the material shaking. "It's quite large and red."

"We also tracked snow inside the cabin. Not to mention, he saw us. He started shooting as soon as we escaped. Don't worry. By now the new snow has covered our tracks. With the temperature dropping, he'll go inside to get out of the cold. We'll find shelter." A line slashed across Moose's forehead. "If he is a killer, as soon as the sun rises, he'll come after us. What criminal wants to let someone who can contact the police get away?"

Either she finally convinced Moose of the danger, or he'd known it all along without admitting it.

"I shouldn't have said that. I was thinking out loud. Please don't start trembling again. We'll find a secure place for tonight, catch some zzz's, and leave tomorrow at first light. An ice storm can disrupt cell phone service here, but maybe we'll get it back soon. Then, we'll contact everyone in the North Carolina Mountains, the police, rescue. You say who. We'll call them."

"That sounds good." Ruthie appreciated Moose's enthusiasm for reaching the authorities, but after all that had happened, it fell flat. She yearned to return to the site of the wrecks and find someone clearing the road. She picked up the thermoses. "Could we go near the highway? I realize we can't stay in our cars if they're still there. If anyone is working in the area tomorrow, we could ask for help though. What do you think?"

Moose shifted his weight. "That's exactly what we'll do. I knew there was a reason I brought you."

"Well, I did pull you through the window."

They laughed and it felt good.

"You're a good kid, Ruthie O'Donnell."

"Thanks." She wasn't sure if she'd grown to trust Moose, or if running from Hucklesford had made her thankful she ended up with Moose—instead of Hucklesford. Of course, Moose was right about the temperature dropping too low for anyone to pursue them now, so there was that. For whatever reason, her anxious muscles unwound. "So, where's a good place to stay between here and there?"

Chapter Three

Ruthie looked at Moose to see how he reacted to her subtle attempt at humor, possibly not appropriate in this white, frozen world, but why not try to make the best of this situation?

"How about the Hilton?"

Ruthie chuckled.

"Seriously, we'll know it when we see it."

"I'm determined to look for it, even though I don't know what or where it is."

She and Moose forged into an arctic blast, Moose pointing his light into the trees to their left, then right.

They all looked the same—like frosty skeletons trying to hide their naked bodies in the fog, except for pine trees with their green needles weighted down. They appeared inverted.

Ruthie pulled her coat tighter. She yearned to sit on a soft sofa in front of a blazing fire, but she would not say that or whine. It would do no good.

After they trudged through an infinity of flurries, Moose stopped and directed the light to the right. "See that huge granite slab frozen in time with water running over it?"

Ruthie peered through the snowflakes. "Yes."

"It forms a hangover resembling a roof. Let's check it out."

Ruthie glimpsed it. "Maybe it would work," she mumbled, more to herself than to Moose. Even if it didn't look like a roof to her, she had no ideas about where to stay. "Okay."

When they reached the site, Ruthie stopped and stared in wonder. With icicles hanging from the trees' branches, the entire silver-tinted side of the hill looked like a crystal wonderland. The cascading waterfall froze into a sculpture of intricate designs against the ice glazed granite. "That's beautiful."

Moose peered down at her and grinned. "Wait until you see it when the sun hits it in the morning, Florida girl."

Ruthie couldn't find one warm place on her. Winter's grip held her toes so tight they refused to wiggle, but the chill couldn't stop her grin. "I see. Like Dorothy and Toto, I'm not in Kansas anymore. Even in this catastrophe, I see the beauty of these mountains." Of course, she saw it. Nothing could dim God's glory. It shone all around them, making this place seem safe. "Let's stay here. We'll camp underneath the slab with the waterfall in front of us, right?"

"Yep."

That would get them out of the elements and break up the wind, especially with the rocks protruding part of the way out of the stone surface behind the waterfall. At least she could rest her tired, aching muscles—maybe.

They finished their walk to the top of the steep grade by holding onto boughs on the trees to steady themselves. When Ruthie saw their campsite, she let out a tiny gasp. It was more than she had hoped for when she raced from the cabin into the unknown. "It's dry."

"I'm sure our floor's frigid, but I have blankets in my football supplies, matches in my personal bag, and winter mountain supplies—not extensive. They don't include a three-course dinner, but we'll manage." Moose unzipped one bag. "We'll have whatever's in your to-go box." He motioned toward Ruthie's leftovers.

"Sure." Ruthie hadn't counted on having a picnic in freezing weather. She sighed. After watching her father eat hearty meals for years, she feared her offering wasn't enough for Moose. At the same time, planning a meal wasn't on her agenda when she left Hilltop. He would have to make do.

"I'm going to find firewood."

Warmth. "Great. I can't wait. If it's all right for me to reach into your bags, I'll spread out the blankets."

"Yeah, go ahead." Moose retrieved another flashlight, passed it to Ruthie, and left.

She rummaged in the luggage until she found two coverlets, one for him and one for her. After she placed them side by side, she sank down on one.

She had trained herself to survive in solitude, to exist in a little corner of the world built for one. She only needed her intellectual pursuits. Her students added variety, so she rarely suffered from boredom. In her free time, she cooked, shopped, cleaned her condo, and read. But this instant, she'd never wanted to see another human being as much as she wanted to see Moose.

The dark sky with clouds hiding the twinkling stars

and moon made the cold, night seem more frigid and lonelier. She clutched the flashlight so tight the stitching on her gloves stretched. With her eyes locked on the bleak landscape, she waited for Moose to break through the tiny beam of light. After a while, the black abyss pulled her into its empty, bottomless pit. As soon as she recognized him heading toward her, she clapped.

His eyes softened in the corners. "Yeah, it's good to see you too." He put down the firewood. "You're shaking again. We're fine here. Don't worry. This will end in the morning. Then we'll go home for Christmas—you to Florida, and me, to the foothills of these mountains. Okay?"

Ruthie swallowed the cold and dark and rose from the depths of despair. She said, "Okay," and hoped he was right.

"I'm starving. Let's build the fire, heat the coffee, and eat," Moose said.

He ripped several pages from a notepad in his football bag. After he added them to a small pile of twigs atop several tree branches, he lit them.

"A glimpse into normalcy." Ruthie took off her gloves and placed her hands near the fire. Her fingers were so cold they were bright pink. Thank goodness, Mom had given her the fuzzy, warm clothes. Her skin probably would've been blue without them.

Moose extracted a sanitary wipe from his bag and ran it around the top of a thermos. "The coffee's compliments of Leroy Banks, the guy who left it in my car. He doesn't drink out of the thermos, but you strike me as an alternative medicine, no-germs-on-me type."

Ruthie laughed. Finally, she and Moose chatted as she'd wanted on the way to the cabin. Now she realized while the chit-chat would've soothed her, Moose had needed to concentrate on getting them out of the cold. "You've got me pegged, but perhaps not as extreme as you think. How about you? What do you do with all of this equipment?"

"I'm the football coach at Hilltop College."

"Honestly. It's my first year there. I'm an English instructor." The association with the college created a touch of familiarity with Moose.

"I see. Only part of a semester wouldn't acclimate a Florida native to these hills."

He sounded friendly. Yet, she'd socialized very little. People could deceive her. She never would have dreamed Runyon Clipz, the senior class president at her high school, would've ended up in prison for embezzling money, but she wasn't going to dwell on Runyon. It wasn't fair to Moose to put his name in the same category as Runyon.

Of course, Moose's size could go in their favor if he ended up in a fistfight with Hucklesford. A chill unrelated to the weather ran down her spine like ice water. Moose would make sure Hucklesford didn't get close enough for the two of them to engage in a skirmish, wouldn't he?

Chapter Four

Ruthie relished the heat from the fire, its red flame flickering in their white world in front of Moose, who drummed his fingers on his knee. She hadn't noticed his long, dark eyelashes and high cheekbones until now. He was quite handsome.

"Hmm. All the books. Do you teach literature?"

"No, advanced grammar."

Moose removed his knit hat and rubbed the top of his head, mussing his short, dark hair. "Man, that stuff drives me nuts."

Ruthie smiled. "Some of my students would agree with you."

"They would, huh? Well, don't pay any attention to them. They're probably football players."

"Football's your world, right?"

"Yep."

"I guess you try to win lots of games."

Moose's eyebrows shot up. "I win 'em all if I can."

Was the will to win in Moose's DNA? They weren't competing in a football game. She hoped he could prevail in the battle with Hucklesford. For all she knew about hiding from criminals, she might as well have been on the moon.

He sipped his coffee and pointed to the thermos. "This taste heavenly. What do you have in the box?"

"Nachos and cheese."

He hunched over. "Is that all? Are they the ones with chili on top?"

"No. Sorry." He was lucky she had these. Letting him think she brought only them would make her other offering exciting. "I also have a hamburger."

Moose raised his arm in the victory sign. "Yes."

"The manager at the diner where I ate lunch will launch a new chili cheeseburger during the Christmas season. He gave me one to try for my opinion." When she looked away from Moose to search in her bag for dinner, the dark deserted forest slapped her in the face. She shivered. The blackness hid bear caves and wolf dens. There were catamounts skulking around, not to mention Hucklesford. Could Moose keep them all away?

Ruthie took a deep breath and turned her attention to their dining area. Ice-glazed granite surrounded her on three sides. Icicles hung off of the ledge in front of her. She might as well have been a vegetable in the freezer. With only the embers from the fire burning now, the campsite grew colder. She pulled her coat tight.

The cheeseburger lay to one side, chili oozing out of it. Even in the brisk air, the aroma wafted around her. The cheesy, greasy smell transported her to the diner, the world she knew. When she set the meal between them, the meager morsels looked small on the blanket. The restaurant beckoned to her from a million miles away.

Moose glanced at the food and flashed a big grin, his thumb turning up in a salute. "Like I said, I'm starving."

Since Ruthie accepted this situation. She had plenty of food for tonight, and tomorrow, they would return to their cars. "I hoped you might have paper plates and napkins in your football bag." He probably didn't, but it didn't hurt to ask.

"No, Ma'am." Moose placed his hand on his bag. "Wait. Yes, I do." He opened it, took out several napkins and handed them to her. "Leroy and I got these this morning at the coffee shop."

She placed a pile of chips on one, gave it to him, then handed him another napkin.

"I'm so hungry I could eat a stick," Moose said.

"Well, you don't have to. Since I'm not a big eater, you can have most of the hamburger."

"No, we'll half it."

His firm tone told Ruthie he wouldn't consider taking more than half.

He reached for it, probably to break it in two pieces.

She shooed his hand away. "I have sanitizer in my purse. Give me a second."

Moose rolled his eyes, but held out his palms while she placed several drops of liquid in them.

Undaunted at his disapproval, Ruthie shot him an intense stare. "Are you a praying man?"

"Yes, I'll say grace." He took Ruthie's hand.

She grew warm. How was that possible in this environment? She glimpsed Moose, then blinked. In a place with so much ice the touch of another human being probably would provide extra body heat. She bowed her head.

"Thank you, dear Lord, for bringing us to a safe place to stay the night and for providing food, especially the hamburger. Please watch over our journey tomorrow, protect us, and take us home to our loved ones for Christmas. In Jesus' name we pray. Amen."

Moose's sweet prayer touched Ruthie. She passed him the burger, which he broke in half. Well, almost. It appeared he did the best he could. She reached for the smaller half.

After they finished eating, Moose cleaned up, placing the empty to-go box and napkins in a plastic bag. "It's too pretty here to litter. I'll dump this in a trashcan when we get to civilization tomorrow."

"Okay." Ruthie wrapped a blanket around her.

Moose held up the other coverlet. "This has padding. We should put it on the bottom. We'll place the one you have on top of us. Similar to the ponchos, now called woobies, used by the military, it's also rain resistant."

"What? You think we're going to get under the same woobie, or whatever it is?"

"Don't worry. I'll stay on my side."

So far, Moose had acted like a gentleman, but she'd find a rock and sleep with it tucked under her in case his character changed in the night. "Do you snore?"

Moose pulled his eyebrows nearly to his nose. "No, but if I did, we don't exactly have an extra room for you."

Ruthie threw up her hands. Just like everything

else she'd confronted since the wreck, she had little choice in the matter unless she wanted to freeze. "Okay, give me the blanket. I'll spread it out." She had not intended the aggravation in her voice, but it flew out.

She eyed a stone not far away from her until Moose lay down on the blanket facing away from her. Then she grasped the rock and clenched it in her fist. Moose probably didn't like this situation any more than she did. They were both victims of a storm and wrecks. She rose on her elbow and studied him, learning no more than he created a large lump.

After twenty minutes Moose asked, "Are you asleep?"

She sacked out in the woods with a man she knew little about. Who knew how many or what kinds of animals roamed near their campsite? Was she asleep? Of course, not. She turned over. "No, I can't. I like to read before I go to bed."

Moose switched on his flashlight and rolled over to face Ruthie. "I go over football plays, then watch the news. Let's chat for a while. Tell me about yourself."

With every ounce of blood inside her, Ruthie yearned for them to survive. Between the hazardous conditions and someone trying to kill them, she had her doubts. Thrown into this perilous situation had made her think about aspects of her life she'd never paid much attention to.

"There's not a lot to tell. Both my parents taught high school until Dad became a principal. They wanted me to pursue the field of education, but they claimed their lives would've been better as college professors. As a result, they insisted I make good grades and qualify for scholarships all the way through grad school."

Moose whistled. "That would've been hard for me. I'm not the studious type."

"I had my nose in a book all the time." She'd accomplished all they had asked. What difference did it make now? Struggling to survive in this wilderness with a killer chasing her, the importance of her degree and the status of it, seemed to matter in a different time and place. Even her dream of having a nice home with a swimming pool, seemed distant. She'd cling to the most important thing Mom and Dad had taught her—to depend on God.

"But you accomplished your…" Moose paused, "…uh, or their goal. Do you like teaching?"

"Yes, my students are a joy. Well, most of them. I sometimes grow weary grading papers, but it's an important part of the job."

Moose propped up his elbow and rested his chin on his fist. "It doesn't sound as though you just love it. I can't imagine myself in another career."

"Did your parents want you to grow up and coach football?"

"I'm not sure."

Ruthie sat up. "How could you not know?"

"My mom wanted me to love my work. My dad's another matter. He was a colonel in the Army. I think he fought too many wars." Moose arched his eyebrows. "Overseas and at home."

"Did he tell you what you should do?"

"He didn't have to. He made it clear I should be just like him. I wanted to be nothing like him."

Ruthie didn't know what to say. It seemed both of them carried a bit of baggage other than their belongings. "You're content now, right?"

"Yes. Where were you going in this ice storm? Home to see the intellectuals?"

"Yeah, were you going to see the colonel and your mom?"

"Yep. They're my family. I'll stay a few days then go back to the college to get ready for our bowl game."

Bowl game. Coaching. What was it Professor Starr, an English instructor at Hilltop, had said about the football team? Ruthie twisted a strand of her hair. "I don't watch a lot of football, but I heard Hilltop College went to the championships this year. Kudos to you."

Moose's big smile shone brighter than the last of the dying embers. "Thanks."

"How'd you get the nickname Moose?"

"Buddies I played with in high school gave it to me." Moose let out a soft chuckle. "It's followed me ever since, but my current competitors call me the evil genius."

Resting and peaceful, Ruthie soaked up the conversation, talking to Moose as easily as she chatted with one of the other English professors. Her ability to relate to Moose puzzled her because they were so different. It must've been because they were the only two humans in this forest who weren't a criminal.

"Do you want to go to sleep now? I'm going to add a few twigs to the fire. I'll watch it until the flames die down."

"Okay." Ruthie couldn't help but fear what tomorrow would bring, but she was exhausted. She rolled over and fell asleep.

Chapter Five

Ruthie awoke to red and yellow colors from the rising sun glinting on ice-covered granite and a crackling fire, but Moose was gone. A lump formed in her throat. He wouldn't leave her, would he? She strained to see him until finally her gaze fell on his gear lying at the bottom of the blanket. Whew! She pulled her duffle bag from his football items just before he appeared.

"If you'd like to freshen up, the bathroom's that way." He pointed to the right.

The snow had stopped, so Ruthie could see his footprints. "Thanks." She snatched her luggage and stepped into the impressions of Moose's large boots to a clearing surrounded by underbrush. Shivering, she tugged on a clean pair of sweatpants and a matching pullover, then returned to their campsite.

Moose had piled up branches for a fire, but he hadn't lit it yet. He squatted down, feeding pieces of dry cereal to a squirrel sitting on a log. The furry little creature perched on his hind legs, his cheeks bulging, his jaws working.

"You must have a way with animals. The little critter looked at ease and so cute." She'd grown up hearing animals recognized good people. That added to her growing trust of Moose.

"They know I like them." He struck a match, lit the fire, and pulled out an individual serving box of cereal from the football gear. "Here, I have one for you."

Ruthie couldn't express her gratitude enough. "Thank you. I'm so hungry."

"You're welcome. I understand." He picked up a branch and lit the end of the stick in the fire. "Go ahead and eat while I melt icicles and fill our thermoses. We should pack up, cover any evidence of our visit, and leave."

Ruthie sat down on the blanket and dug into the box as she gazed at the wintry forest. The silvery trees in the distance sparkled like diamonds, but to the left, she noticed a different scene. The sun's rays reflected off of...what? She squinted her eyes. Was it Hucklesford?

She pulled on Moose's coat sleeve. "Look over there." She pointed toward the left with a shaky forefinger. "The man with the binoculars."

Moose slapped his forehead. "I must've taken us in a circle." He snatched items, stuffing them in the bags.

Ruthie shoved her belongings into her bag with trembling hands.

After Moose threw snow onto the fire until it stopped sizzling, he took Ruthie by the arm. "Let's go."

Could Moose find his way back to the site of their accidents? Could he really protect them from a killer? She couldn't do either. How could they escape these woods or Hucklesford? A chill as cold as the air ran through her. She pulled her cell phone from her purse and tapped it.

Moose pulled her along. "I checked. There's no signal. We can try again when we're farther away from him."

"Do you think he saw us?"

Shots fired in the distance.

"Yeah."

Ruthie tightened her steps. "We're walking downhill, the incline's getting steeper, and…and it's snowing again."

"You're right about all of that."

Moose had only suggested they go to the cabin because he'd gone hunting around here with his dad. "Do you know where we are?"

"Not really."

More gunfire pierced the air.

"He's firing from farther away."

Ruthie didn't tell Moose how angry she was. It wasn't his fault there was an ice storm. He tried to help their situation. "As I recall, we didn't go up a hill to reach the cabin. Yet, you said we walked toward the highway. How's that possible? We're going down a steep slope." Weakness swept over her. "I have to sit down."

"No. We can't. A murderer wants our hide. Remember."

She sank to the ground. "I don't hear the shots or footsteps anymore."

Moose pulled her up. "That's because it's snowing. The snow won't crunch until it freezes, but we should stay so far away from him he can't hit us."

Ruthie moaned. If Hucklesford didn't kill her, the

terrain and this bitter weather would. She'd inherited her mother's stoic attitude and her father's determined will. Neither had prepared her for facing a frozen forest challenging her to conquer a hard, icy surface or die.

Suddenly the trees closed in on her. Their hoary color struck by specs of sunlight spun. She tried to move through the fog as a strong wind sucked her into a freezing abyss. No way out.

A jerk yanked her to safety. She faced Moose's black jacket. He steadied her and took a step backward. "I'm sorry. I know I messed up."

She lunged into his arm with her fists. "We're lost, and it's your fault. We're never getting out of here. They'll find us with the dead squirrels and raccoons with the spring thaw, unless that madman shoots us first."

~

Growing up, Moose had taken the blame for mistakes that weren't his fault, rather than make his life more difficult by arguing about them with his domineering father. As a young adult, he realized, he didn't have to carry the burden, which had become a part of him. Instead, he thought through a situation and analyzed it to decide whether he'd made the misstep.

"I'm a football coach, not a mountain guide." Moose thrust out his chest. "I know enough to keep us warm and dry though. When my father and I spent time in these woods, he taught me wilderness skills. This morning, I woke early and pointed my left arm toward the sun. Then I held my right one to the west. I should've faced south. I'm not sure what went wrong. Maybe the highway isn't south."

"Why didn't you at least tell me? Surely, you must

feel some responsibility for this disaster."

Moose clenched his fist, digging his nails into his palms. After all he'd done to keep Ruthie safe, his blood boiled. She wasn't his responsibility. Clearly, the only grateful woman he knew was his mother. If it weren't for her and his Christian beliefs he might explode. He sniffed like a bull. Ruthie needed to learn some self-restraint. He gazed down at her, ready to tell her she should take classes in anger management. She looked so pitiful. "I can understand your frustration with me, but it won't solve our problem."

Ruthie tightened her mouth. "No, it won't, and unfortunately, we have no way of resolving this mess."

"We'll think of something. I know one thing. Even though we can't always hear Hucklesford and sometimes we can't see through the fog, he's stayed behind us." He peered at Ruthie. She was listening. "If I'm right, and I think I am, he still is. That means he won't suddenly fire at us from the left or right, or meet us head on if we keep going forward. Another thing, the weather will slow him down, just as it does us. He won't stay on our heels because he can't. If he continues to pursue us, he'll have to get out of the cold at night then find us the next day. We have an advantage."

"Okay, let's put our effort into staying so far ahead of him he won't know where we are."

"You got it. We should leave right away." Neither of them could afford to debate who was at fault for what. They had to survive.

Ruthie put her hands over her face. "I'm sorry. There's no telling how many people died in the rockslide, how many cars went over the cliff at that dangerous curve, or how many froze in their cars. We are alive because you kept us from freezing and dodged a killer."

Her words sent Moose's spirits soaring like a bird that hit a window, then realized it could still fly. A woman from Florida certainly had few to no options in these elements with a criminal chasing her, but for a reason Moose didn't understand he yearned for Ruthie to want to go with him. He looked into her sad green eyes and wanted to see them light up. "We *will* stay ahead of the man brandishing a weapon. Let's go."

Now, to get them down the mountainside and see what lay in the dell. As they walked, Moose waited for Ruthie to say something. Was she exhausted? Discouraged? Until now, she hadn't hesitated to tell him.

Finally, she asked, "Do you think the police sent a search party into the woods?"

Moose hated to disappoint her, to tell her the truth. "If the roads were open for an hour or more during the warmest part of the day, I imagine the police and rescue units approached the scene of the accident from the south. They probably discovered our vehicles and those that..." Moose swallowed a lump of sadness in his throat. "We weren't the only ones leaving the college that day. If history is any indicator, some of them went over."

"But they'll see our empty cars, realize we're missing, and try to find us, right?"

"During the daylight hours, sure."

Guilt rippled over Moose's skin. Deep down, he questioned the validity of his words because the first responders would focus on survivors at the scene and bring up the deceased from the bottom of the cliff. Who knew though? Maybe someone combed part of the woods.

The edges of Ruthie's lips spread into a beautiful smile. "Good. I expect they'll rescue us soon."

If only that were true. Moose bit his tongue.

As they walked farther down the slope, each of their steps landed on topography more vertical than the last. Ruthie skidded.

"Hold a low-hanging tree branch before you take a stride."

"Sounds good. Going down such a steep incline, I'm beginning to think I'm part mountain goat."

Moose couldn't stop laughing. Finally, he spoke between muffled chuckles. "You're full of surprises, but I don't believe you have any goat in you. You know your animals though. This area isn't fit for much else."

"What about catamounts?"

Moose didn't want to tell her they lurked around canyons searching for a meal. "Well, I don't see any."

"Are we likely to see one?"

A whizz shot past them. Moose jerked Ruthie to him. A thud cracked ice to their side. One of the fierce creatures lay dead, blood oozing from its head.

Ruthie screamed.

Moose cleared his throat of the anxiety stuck in it. "That gun blast probably frightened all the catamounts in this area. More than likely, they're running away, so we don't need to worry about them. We should get out of the shooter's sight."

"Someone could hunt for food or recreation in this kind of weather, couldn't they?"

"It's not impossible, but unlikely. Even if a person

needed food, he'd probably choose a better time to look for it."

"I'm going as fast as I can. The tree limbs support my body, but my feet are flying out from under me."

Moose couldn't hold the urgency in any longer. "Do the best you can and pray."

No sooner had Moose told Ruthie to do the best she could than the branch she held onto split, and she lost her balance, tumbling down the hill.

"Help. Help." She picked up speed, rolling faster and faster.

Moose's heart raced. He snatched hold of one bough after another, tapping the ground with his toes, swinging to the next limb in mid-air to reach the bottom, hoping to find her alive.

Chapter Six

Ruthie landed in a pile of snow in a valley. The spinning sensation she experienced on the roundabout as a child hit her. The treetops on the mountains surrounding her whirled around and around as she sat up in a swirling world. She lay down. After three tries, she rose up and checked for broken bones. Moving without pain, she let out a sigh of relief. *Dear Lord, thank you for carrying me down that hill.*

Huffing and puffing, Moose charged to her, threw down the bags, and embraced her. "Are you okay?"

"Yes, I'm fine."

"Thank goodness, you rolled and fell in soft snow. Still, you could've landed in a bad position and broken a bone. I'm sorry you fell. I'm sorry I brought us into this forest."

"No. Don't say that. It's better than staying in a vehicle teetering on the edge of a cliff."

Moose's eyes doubled in size. He took hold of her hand and squeezed it. "God willing, I'll get us out of here safe and sound. What happened up there?"

"When the bough broke, I couldn't grab another one fast enough." Ruthie focused heavenward. "Do you believe in miracles?"

Moose bowed his head, then raised it. "Yes, I do, why?"

"Little everyday miracles?"

"Yes, those too. Even if you fell in snow, and it's softer than ice, it's a wonder you didn't break something, right?"

"No. There's a reason I fell. In the distance, I may have spotted a house. I fell down the hill so fast, it's hard to know for sure. I don't see it now, but it was over there." She pointed to their right. "Did I imagine it, or did God show it to me for an instant?"

"I don't know, but that's as good of a direction to take as any. Since you noticed it from a different vantage point, it's possible we can't see it from here."

Ruthie pushed up.

Before she stood, Moose motioned for her to stay put. "Rest for a few minutes."

"What about Hucklesford? With only a few trees and no leaves to hide us, we're exposed."

"If he attempts to follow us, he won't tumble to the bottom of that steep grade on purpose. You bought us a little time." Moose caressed her forearm, his touch light. "I'm sorry for what it cost."

"Whew." Ruthie blew out her fear. "If only we had something to eat."

"We do." Moose spread a blanket between them. Reaching in his football bag, he said, "Wait until you see this." He pulled out two individual boxes of cereal. "And we have..."

"Protein powder. I can't thank you enough."

Moose handed her the cereal and mixed their drinks. Then he said grace.

Ruthie gulped down the cereal. Even though it was a meager meal, it was a blessing. "I'm not a social dining partner. I'm so hungry I can't think of an interesting topic."

"No need to. I can't think of anyone I'd rather eat with. It was the perfect time to have a meal. We need to move on though."

Ruthie held up her thermos. "We'll have to find more icicles to melt to fill these."

"That's easy. There's more foliage on the other side of this valley." Moose turned up his thermos, emptying his drink.

Ruthie pulled her cell phone out of her purse. "I know from everything you've said about the weather interrupting service this probably won't work. I have to try though. I don't doubt for one second my parents are worried. I imagine the police in Florida and North Carolina have heard earfuls from them."

She tried. Nothing happened. She tried again. Tears built deep inside where reality had kicked her. She blinked her eyelids as fast as she could to keep from crying.

"I'm sure my parents are concerned too. Since I'm a man, my dad thinks I can take care of myself. My mom will never believe that. Hopefully, she isn't too upset." Moose stood. "Let's find that house you saw."

Ruthie got up as Moose gathered the bags. "Since there's a frozen lake somewhere out here, we need to find solid ground to cross to the other side."

Ruthie picked up the thermoses and stepped into a world of white that appeared to go to infinity. Only the blue tinted sky and an occasional scrawny tree reminded her she was on earth. "This forsaken area with a lake makes me think of Clyde Griffiths killing his girlfriend in *An American Tragedy*, even though he didn't do it in the winter. If he had, the story couldn't have happened the way it did. I'm rambling on and on about literature. I guess I'm so cold I'm trying to keep my brain warm."

"I understand. Clyde's the character who wants to get his poor girlfriend out of the way because he has something going with a high society woman. He takes her out on a lake, and she falls in, right?"

Moose knew more about literature than he let on. "Yes."

He puckered his mouth as though he ate something that tasted bad. "He does nothing and watches her drown. Geez, what a sleazeball."

"Wow! For a football coach, you know your novels."

"Not really. Our freshman lit professor insisted we read *An American Tragedy* and present a speech about it." Moose let out a soft snort. "It's a good thing you brought *it* up. It's the only one I studied in depth. I'm neither a student of literature nor an eloquent speaker. I'm a football coach."

"Well, you nailed that one. I know nothing about football. Tell me something."

"Okay. You've heard of the quarterback?"

"Sure. Were you one?"

"No. I was a linebacker."

Ruthie sighed. "Sorry."

"It's our jobs to keep the players on the other team from scoring or making a first down." Moose looked at Ruthie. "A first down is a ten-yard advancement. If our opponent doesn't move the ball ten yards in three plays, they have to kick it to us. Technically, it's called a punt." Ridges formed on Moose's forehead. "Well, they have one more option. If they'd rather not punt, they can go for it." Moose peered down at her.

Even though she tried to understand his explanation, it made no sense.

"If they go for it and don't make ten yards, we get the ball right there."

Ruthie didn't want to tell Moose he might as well have spoken Chinese for all she learned about first downs and punts. The way he loved that sport, she doubted they could be friends if she knew nothing about linebackers? "The team goes down the field ten yards. Go on."

Moose's eyebrows shot up. "The linebackers can knock down the quarterback, cover the receivers, intercept the ball, and tackle runners."

Try as hard as she could, Ruthie failed to comprehend what it meant to be a linebacker. She drew her features tight.

Moose glanced at her. "I'll tell you what, when we return to school, come over and watch a game with me. I'll explain what happens as they play. Then, you can let me know how you like the sport."

Ruthie stumbled. Was he asking her for a date? After the past couple of days, she wouldn't worry about spending time with him. She'd like it. She'd agree for now, see if he followed through later. "Okay."

Satisfaction danced in Moose's eyes.

It was a date. Anticipation colored her white world with beautiful shades of hope. As she walked with rose petals swirling in her brain, her tired body seemed lighter. She and Moose would escape this foray into the wilderness, emerge victorious, and see normalcy once again.

She walked tall until she heard crunches. Looking for a place to hide, she glanced right and left, then at Moose. "Hucklesford?"

He stopped walking and turned around. "Yeah, more than likely. I'm sure he doesn't want us to tell the authorities someone lives in a deserted, old cabin in the woods, let alone, that he shot at us."

Ruthie peered down at her coat. "If it wasn't for my button..."

"Stop worrying about the button. You didn't lose it on purpose. You sound like me on one of my guilt trips."

"You have those too?"

"Well, uh, yeah, I do. I'm dealing with it though. About the button, with everything happening in that cabin, no one would've noticed it missing. When I heard those footfalls on the porch, I didn't say, 'Gee, let me check to see if a button's fallen off of my coat.' Hucklesford had to realize someone had been there. We left the window open, and..."

"What if he fired at us because he saw the button? I've been telling myself he didn't."

"Keep it up until you convince yourself."

"And silly me, I hoped the shots came from someone hunting dinner." Ruthie slapped her cheek. She had come a long way in more ways than one since they left their cars on the highway. "I know better now."

Moose got an empty stare. "I know you do. I hate that. I hate this situation, but here we are. We have to keep moving forward, especially now. We stand out like flashing neon lights in this hollow."

Ruthie sped up, her breath coming in frosty spurts. Never worrying about getting killed before, she yearned to live, really live, not just exist.

"Slow down before you fall again."

"I heard something behind us."

Chapter Seven

Moose tried to churned like someone stirred it. "Ruthie."

She kept racing over the frozen lake.

Moose peered at his boots. Would they grip the ice? Would the ice hold him if he had to walk on it.? What about weak spots? Only a fair swimmer in summer in water heated by the sun, could he swim at all in these conditions? He shook, and not from the cold. He had to calm down.

If she fell, he'd navigate to the hole where she disappeared and anchor something to show him that spot. He grabbed his football bag and rummaged through it with trembling hands, pushing socks, sweatpants, and bandaging tape to one side. A bright purple shirt T-shirt. Praying he wouldn't need the shirt, he put the leftovers back in the bag.

~

What did Moose say? Ruthie squinted to see him. The two of them were targets on Hucklesford's shooting range. They had to find a path to the other side of the hollow and build a campsite before nightfall. Why was Moose taking his time? What was wrong with him? He should pick up his pace.

He said something again, louder. Ruthie stumbled at his words. Wait. Did he find shelter for the night? She couldn't imagine how or where amid nothing but open space. Moose could do pretty incredible things though. She walked in his direction.

He beckoned, his hands waving frantically while he screamed, "Stay focused on me."

If he needed her, she'd be there for him. She sped up. Slipping. Sliding. Only a few feet now.

The ice gave way. Her pulse thrashed in her temples. She grabbed the rim of the opening.

It broke. She sank into the cold water.

Find something to grab. Another piece of ice. She swung her arms in wild motions as tremors wracked her body. She twisted. Nothing to hang onto, water pulling her down. She pedaled her feet.

Sinking. Sinking. She forced her body up, didn't she? An inch? A half an inch?

No, she fell deeper into dark nothingness. Smothering. Drowning. No way out. A cement block spiraling in heartless water with no escape. Courage. Think. She kicked and pulled, then drifted down in the frigid lake. If only she had more air in her lungs, she'd fight the bitter, dark monster.

~

Moose charged to the hole in the ice like a freight train. He dropped to his knees at the opening that swallowed Ruthie, rammed his shoulders underwater, and swooshed his arms like propellors. Tears puddled in his eyes. The space blurred. *Oh please, God, let me get hold of her before it's too late.*

He leaned farther into the lake, his chin bobbing up

and down in the icy water. Nauseated, he gagged. Still, he forced his upper body deeper into the abyss. Out of air, he had to sit up. Spitting spray from the lake, he coughed.

He shoved his numb hands into the liquid deathtrap. Swished them over and over. Found a sloshing void. He pulled out, folded his knees underneath him, and gasped for air. The cavity was too small. He leaned farther into the ice. It cracked around him. He swished his arms back and forth, leaned farther into the hole. Tried again. Nothing but water.

He was going in. He lunged deeper and touched something. He grabbed it and tugged with all his might—Ruthie's coat.

He pulled her up, energy racing through him like electricity, joy for her life filling him from head to toe. In moments, he laid her on the ice. It cracked. He pulled her toward the shore, dragging her like a soldier wounded in battle. Fracturing ice with each step, he walked fast, barely staying in front of the surface breaking behind them.

Finally, he reached solid ground. Ruthie blinked. She was alright. She had to be alright. He placed her face down, pulled the blankets from his bag, and wrapped one around her. "You're okay. You're okay. You couldn't have been under more than several seconds. I was right there. You have to be okay. Wake up. Wake up. Oh, please wake up and say something. I brought you with me because it was the right thing to do. But, it's so much more. So much more. Please. Please. You have to be alright."

Ruthie coughed. "I'm..." she sputtered and spit out water. "Okay." Her voice sounded hoarse, but she was conscious.

"Thank goodness, the wind's not blowing. We have to warm you. Are you too weak to sit up?" He lifted Ruthie.

Shivering, Ruthie answered, "No-no, I'm fine, just fre-freezing." She wiped sodden, strawberry blonde curls from her face. "I dropped the thermos bottles in the water."

"They don't matter, just you. You need to get dry as soon as possible. Take off those clothes." He tried to sound calm, but he would burst if she didn't do as he asked right away. "I'm going to turn around, find what you need, and throw the items over my shoulder. Let me know when you're dressed."

"Okay. You should change your clothes too."

"I will, but you first. Do it." Moose didn't want to tell Ruthie the awful things that could happen if she didn't get dry soon. His nerves did a war dance for wanting her to hurry.

"You look like a cat after a bath. You're going to get frostbite."

"Just put on the clothes." Moose emphasized each word using his father's firmest military tone. "Now." Facing away from her, he reached in his bag and threw out a pair of thermal leggings, a large pullover, shoes with cleats, along with three pairs of heavy wool socks. Then he flung a heavy sweatpants suit and a sweater from her bag. "Get these on." He flipped her a towel. "Squeeze as much water out of your hair as possible. I have another wool hat I'll loan you."

"All right."

A brisk wind hit Moose's saturated coat. Biting dampness seeped into his pores. He trembled from head to toe.

"I'm dressed." Ruthie turned around. "You're shaking. Take the blanket." Ruthie held it out.

"Ye-ye-yes. My-my teeth are chat-chat chattering. Thank you."

"Get dry clothes now. Get the other coverlet and use it."

"You're going to wear it. Your coat's drenched."

"Well, do something before you go into shock or have hypothermia. I have no idea what to do for either." Ruthie's voice trailed off.

"We have five or ten minutes before that sets in. Don't worry." Moose started peeling off his coat.

Ruthie turned around. "Change fast. I'm not looking."

Moose threw down his overcoat and yanked off his sweater and T-shirt, along with his socks and shoes, then tossed them on top of Ruthie's soaked clothes. He quickly pulled two wool sweaters, a jacket, a pair of thermal leggings, sweatpants, wool socks, and shoes from his football bag.

He tugged them on, then put his hand on Ruthie's shoulder. "I have mittens. They're too big for your small hands, but they'll work."

After she put them on, he placed the knit hat on her head and chuckled. "It comes all the way to your nose."

~

Ruthie removed the hat and held it close to her chest. She was alive. Joy raced through her like a raging river. She wanted to live. From now on, she'd make every day count for good, for happiness, for doing God's will. She would no longer exist on the edge of life in her own bubble. She put the hat on. "I love this.

Thank you for loaning it to me."

"You're welcome."

Moose placed all the clothes in his soppy coat lying on the snow and tied the sleeves. No sooner did he pick up the garments than the dripping water started to freeze. Pushing the bundle away from him, he knitted his eyebrows.

Ruthie pulled a plastic garbage bag from her items. "Believe it or not, I carry these on trips to hold my laundry. Stuff the wet clothes in here."

~

"Good thinking." Moose had never known the type of affection radiating through him as he looked down at Ruthie. He'd come so close to losing her. The anguish of seeing her slip into that hole in the ice had wracked every muscle and bone in him.

He'd stopped dating after his relationship with a woman the kids on the team had called the bomb. She tried to order him around, had the answers to everything. Anyone who disagreed with her fell into the idiot category. Not only that, she acted like a brat. The night he cooked steaks on the grill, she claimed he didn't know how to choose a good one.

He said, "I paid a small fortune for it."

She threw her knife on the plate and shouted, "How do you expect me to eat this? If I'm not good enough to take to a decent restaurant for an evening out, I'm not good enough to date you." She'd stomped out of his house. He'd always thought there was more to it than the steak. It wasn't that tough.

"It's twilight. What are we going to do now?" Ruthie's sweet voice brought Moose to the moment.

"I'm not sure yet, but I'm working on it." After he

got them out of this forest safely, he intended to learn more about Ruthie. He'd make sure she enjoyed the evening watching the football game at his house and go from there.

"I have no doubt you'll think of something."

Chapter Eight

Ruthie plodded along, making sure she kept five feet between her and the frozen lake. Relieved neither she nor Moose showed any signs of frostbite, she looked heavenward. "Thank you." Then she gazed at Moose. "I'm grateful for your help and quick thinking."

"Of course, I don't want anything to happen to you."

"I'm sorry I caused so much trouble."

"You're excused since you're from Florida. I guess you don't have many frozen lakes there."

Ruthie shook her head. If only she could shake the guilt. "I'll think of some way to make it up to you."

Moose put his arm around Ruthie's shoulders. "We're okay."

Ruthie pondered Moose's words. She could live with them, at least until she could redeem herself. She itched to get out of this wilderness and start her new life. She planned to squeeze all the fun and friendship she could out of each second of every day. If Moose mentioned the football game after they returned to Hilltop, she would say yes immediately. "Is this called

Endless Lake?"

Moose chuckled. "I don't know the name."

"You don't know where we are?"

Moose let out a loud sigh. "Ruthie, I'm trying."

"I'm teasing. You're doing a great job. I'm the one who nearly drowned because I tried to cross an iced-over lake and caused you to nearly freeze to death."

"Wandering in desolate territory with everything camouflaged by winter can create a loss of direction and perspective."

Ruthie looked up at Moose. "I really regret my careless abandon. I got upset because we have nowhere to stay for the night."

"Yeah. I know. All's well now." Moose pointed to the trees in the distance. "I'm hoping and praying we find a way over there before dark."

Ruthie intended to do everything in her power to tackle these elements. For the first time since they slept underneath the waterfall in the dark in this cold forsaken place, the horror seemed survivable with Moose by her side. "I haven't heard any footsteps. No one's shooting at us."

"As we determined, you put some distance between us and Hucklesford when you rolled down that hill. He'll do all he can to catch up, but look ahead." He pointed to a spot. "The lake appears narrower. Maybe we can cross there."

Was he kidding? "I can't step on that body of water again."

"You won't. We'll find a safe place to walk over."

There was nothing safe about the swirling threat to life and limb lurking underneath the ice. "I need somewhere I can't fall in the lake?"

"The location we're headed toward looks like a snow-covered path or a bridge of some sort."

"I don't see it."

Moose gave Ruthie a half grin. "Don't worry. You can handle whatever we find."

Moose trusted her. She stepped a little lighter. She would cope—somehow. "Like everything else since I wrecked my car, I don't have a choice."

As the sun started to sink from the sky, Moose picked up his pace.

Ruthie did the same. When the heavens grew gray, she surveyed the never-ending landscape of ice and snow.

Moose rummaged in his bag until he got out the flashlight and two thermoses. Then he handed the thermos bottles to Ruthie. "Here ya' go."

"I was worried about losing the ones in the lake."

"No problem. I had extra."

"Now, if we only had somewhere to stay."

"We will."

Ruthie hung the thermoses on her wrists.

Moose swung his flashlight to his right, left, and around in circles before he focused on the right spot. "There."

Ruthie clenched her teeth as she forced her feet to keep pace with Moose, who hurried over the slippery terrain. As they drew close, she recognized a ten-foot-wide beavers' dam over a reedy portion of the lake.

Moose winked at her. "As long as we don't disturb the critters' lodge, I don't think they'll care if we use the dam."

Ruthie pulled her knit cap farther down covering her ears. "What are those things made of?"

"Logs, woven sticks, grass, and moss held together with mud. It will support us. Wild animals, like bears when they aren't hibernating, walk across them. Not only does this one look sturdy, it's the best possibility to reach the other side we've seen in hours."

Sturdy? It looked rickety, but Ruthie had confidence in Moose. She would take his word for the durability of their proposed bridge. And once again, what choice did she have? "Let's go for it."

"We won't disturb the little critters. They usually sleep during the day and go out at night." Moose pointed to the dam. "You go first. I'm right behind you."

"Okay."

Moose handed Ruthie a flashlight. After she lit up the dam, she stepped onto it with one foot, placed the other carefully, and continued. Balancing with her arms, she kept a steady gait, concentrating only on getting across—until she no longer heard footsteps behind her. Did Moose fall? Nothing broke the silence.

"I tripped, but I'm fine. Don't look back. Keep going."

Ruthie's foot slipped. She gasped. The chill of the lake crept over her. Barely able to speak, she whispered, "Anything but another dip in the cold water. I want safe passage. I don't need to hurry." She strained to see through the fog, nearly smothering her. The trees on the other side appeared like phantoms in the mist. How much farther would it take to reach them? Even though she tried to plant her feet securely, she trembled with each step. She slipped again. Her nerves buckled.

"Don't panic." Moose's voice rang out.

She wiggled her foot onto the dam, then plodded

forward with every muscle in her body twisted in a tight knot.

"We're almost there." He flashed the light to the other side.

Ruthie made out boughs on the trees, even specs of green in the pines. "Yes." She yelled in delight as she picked up her pace. Her foot slid into a sharp twig, ripping her sweatpants and leggings. Red droplets fell onto white ice. A sinking sensation swept through her. Lifting the injured limb, she called on every ounce of strength she had to keep from yelling. Stings, aches, and throbbing ricocheted through her.

"Don't look down. You're doing great."

Ruthie hated what she had to do, but Moose's words encouraged her as she continued across the dam, inhaling, exhaling, hoping not to pass out. Even though she writhed in pain, she refused to faint and tumble off of the dam into the dark, freezing, life-sucking water, no matter how much it hurt.

"Hang in there." Moose's voice sounded far away.

What did he say? He needed her to keep moving.

"Just a little farther. You can do it. We have to get to the other side."

Getting off of this dam, no matter what it cost, meant she wouldn't drown in the water below and she and Moose could escape a killer one more night. She took slow steps, her foot and leg quivering, the wintry world swirling as the fog and ice pulled her in.

"You can do it." Reassurance rang in Moose's voice, but it sounded faint. She was still on the dam. The shore blurred. She couldn't think straight. How much farther? She needed to lie down.

Tortured, she fell into a daze. A force inside her

walked for her to the end of the dam. She recalled nothing after taking a step on the other side of the frozen lake. Then warmth wrapped around her.

She moaned and gazed about.

Moose held her, the muscles in his face tight as he placed her on glacial terrain then lay down beside her. He reached over and squeezed her hand. "It's too late and too cold for Hucklesford to come after us now. Once we find somewhere to stay, we can rest. First, we need to see about your wound."

The word rest repeated over and over like a stuck CD in Ruthie's brain. Moose sat up, lifted her upright, and held her. "Soon I'll make a fire. We'll get a good night's sleep." He peered at her ankle and leg and grimaced. "Get that sock off before blood freezes on it. I have several more pairs. One of the beavers must've chewed the stick that cut you into a sharp point."

Moose's embrace settled Ruthie into the moment, even with pain ripping through her. She had to stay brave because they needed to cope with much more than a nasty cut near her ankle. She dug deep inside and pushed words beyond the dizziness. "That football bag must have a bottomless pit."

A smile flickered on Moose's lips as he got out alcohol, antibiotic ointment, band-aids and non-stick pads. "Besides first aid supplies, it holds my gear, plus the players constantly ask me to keep stuff for them."

Moose rambled on about the water bottles and thermoses as though he chattered to distract her. She appreciated his efforts, but his words sounded like noise in the background of the pain yelling at her.

He gave her a bag of cotton balls and a small bottle of alcohol. "Wash it with this first."

Ruthie rubbed the disinfectant over the hurt place. "Ouch."

Moose passed her the gel. "This won't burn."

She applied the ointment to the gash on her ankle before placing a non-stick pad and tape over it, then she handed the supplies to Moose. "Thanks."

He gave her a big hug. "There, that's not so bad, right?"

Even though her ankle throbbed, Ruthie nodded. Thanks to Moose and his first aid kit, her wound probably wouldn't get infected.

He offered her some leftover medical supplies. "Keep these, so you can change the dressing each morning until your boo-boo heals."

Ruthie placed the material in her sweatpants pocket as Moose scanned the area. What would she do without Moose? If only he had taken them to the highway, but she couldn't dwell on what might have been. She might have gone over the cliff too. "I appreciate all you've done. I've never officially thanked you for saving me twice."

Moose smiled. "No problem. You're going to make it up to me watching football." He stood and picked up the bags.

Ruthie grasped the thermos bottles. "We better get going to stay ahead of Hucklesford. I'm convinced he's not going to stop chasing us until he's shot us, or we've escaped. I suppose he might leave us alone if he believed we had no idea who he is. Honestly, the ironic thing—we don't know who he is."

"We'll hope for the best scenario, but prepare for the worst."

Moose shined the flashlight on the wintry forest,

then they trekked deeper into unknown territory with no sign of a waterfall with a slab of granite for a roof, or even a spot underneath a cluster of pine trees.

Ruthie's injured ankle ached. Every bone in her body cried for rest. She tried to form a word to start a conversation with Moose, but exhausted, she couldn't. It didn't matter. He probably suggested they'd watch football together to soothe her. When they returned to the campus, he'd hang out with the other coaches and his players. She'd mix with that bunch like oil with water. Even though she'd hung out with those in the church youth group and the English and Communication Clubs, she'd gone on only a few dates in college and had had no serious boyfriends.

She'd been living underneath the ice over a lake her entire life. God had given her a chance for happiness. She would take it. "What do you like to do when you aren't coaching?"

"Watch football."

"Do you have any other interests?"

"Not many. I attend church. I enjoy going out for a meal or a burger. Love burgers."

"I have filet burgers in my freezer. When I come to watch the game, would you like me to bring them?"

"You bet. I'll grill them."

Even though Ruthie counted more on the date not happening than she did on Moose

keeping it, she sent him a big grin. "It's a deal."

He shined the flashlight to their right. "I saw a cave. Did you?"

Interested in Moose, Ruthie hadn't noticed her surroundings. "No, I'm sorry."

Moose walked a few paces to the right. "There it

is." He lit up the entrance.

"Eww. I imagine it's nasty in there. What about bats and bears?"

Chapter Nine

Ruthie examined the dirt and moss entrance to the cave and peeked inside at the brownish-yellow stalactites and stalagmites. She wanted to like this place. Her aching wounds and tired body wanted her to like it. "Do they have rockslides in caves?"

Moose tapped his foot. "I suppose it's possible, but we shouldn't get trapped. Most caves have more than one opening. Let's find the other exit."

"What if there's a bear hibernating and we wake him?"

"I'll check. You wait here."

Ruthie marched in place, trying to stop a shiver, and it wasn't from the temperature. "I'll go too."

Moose turned, motioned for her to come on.

She gritted her teeth. If they met a scary creature, she was ready to run on a moment's notice, even with a hurt ankle. "I've read bears sometimes wake up and roam around during their dormant state."

"If we see one, we won't disturb him if he's sleeping. If he's wandering about, we'll get outta' here fast."

Even though Ruthie worried they couldn't get out of the cave faster than a bear, getting out of the cold, ice, and frozen snow appealed to her. She walked beside Moose for what seemed like miles before moonlight washed over a second entrance. Her muscles relaxed. "I've scanned this place with eagle eyes. It appears safe as long as there aren't any bats."

"They won't bother you if you don't bother them. This place will protect us from the bitter weather," Moose said.

Ruthie nodded, then said, "But I can't sleep with bats."

Moose let out a loud sigh. "Not all caves have them. If there are any, they usually hang around the entrances. There are none here."

"Are bats birds or rodents?" If the ugly things were birds, they might not disgust her as much.

Moose placed his hands on his hips. "In our dire situation, I can't believe you want to know the classification of a bat. It must be a spin-off of the detail oriented, advanced grammarian coming out in you. I wouldn't know except for Jordan, a football player on the team, who explores caves. They're of the Chiroptera order, the only flying mammal, according to him. Still worried?"

"Whatever. It doesn't matter. They're creepy." She probably wouldn't have liked them any better if they'd been birds. She turned on the flashlight Moose had given her at the dam and scrutinized each spot on the inside of the cave's entryway. "Okay, if there are none at the other end, I'll stay here." She pretended she had leverage, even though it seemed less likely every time Moose spoke. "The place isn't too bad. It smells a little musty and a bit like dirt, but honestly, the air's fresher than I imagined."

"Jordan says caves have large and small openings, so air circulates pretty well." He looked around. "We can rest here. I'd welcome a good night's sleep."

In spite of her throbbing ankle, Ruthie walked faster. She fanned herself. What if there were bats at the other entrance? Could they get away before one bit them? On their trek to the other end of the cavern, she glimpsed water flowing beside her, but paid little attention to it. She put all of her energy into spotting a bat, wild animal, hair-raising insect, or any other predator. "It appears we're the only ones with reservations."

Moose chuckled, a bit of relief ringing in his laughter.

Ruthie kept silent. He'd convinced her to stay here one evening. She hoped he didn't expect her to rest easy. If he did, he had a bit more convincing to do.

"I'll look for logs and sticks to build a fire." He touched Ruthie's garbage bag with the toe of his boot. "While I'm gone, dig out the wet clothes. We'll dry them."

"Sure thing."

After Moose left, Ruthie peered into the darkness and loneliness whipped around her like a stiff wind. With a trembling finger, she switched on the flashlight, then surveyed their mountain motel for a way to dry the garments. "Yes." If she removed the strings from the waist of her and Moose's wet sweatpants and tied them together, she could make a clothesline. Within thirty minutes, she fastened one of their drawstrings to two protruding rocks, one on the right wall, the other on the left. Even though the faux clothesline hung uneven, it worked. Finally, she had done something helpful other than supply one hamburger and pull Moose through half of a French door.

He entered, glanced at her handiwork. "Hi, what's going on?"

"I made a clothesline, but I don't know what to do with the coats."

"We could hang them on the rocks. Even if we can't spread them out, they'll dry faster than they will in a wad in the bag."

"Yeah." Ruthie grinned. "Maybe I'm becoming an outdoors woman."

Moose winked at her. "Could've fooled me. I thought you already were one."

"Hardly, I nearly killed us trying to walk across that frozen lake."

"But we're fine."

Thanks to Moose.

She had hung a clothesline. If she really tried, she could do more.

After he started the fire, they sat on a blanket in front of it.

"It's a shame we can't roast something good for dinner, like a hamburger." Moose threw up his hands as if to ask, why us?

"Roasted cereal?"

Moose fingered the sleeve of his jacket. "Jordan says some caves have underground waterways with blind fish swimming in them. Are we that lucky? Of course not."

Ruthie liked fish. "Do they come with tartar sauce or ketchup?"

Moose hooted.

"Ah, guess what? I saw water on the way back

from the other end of the cave. Going that way, it's on our left."

Moose sprang up.

Ruthie could taste her dinner.

Moose led the way, lighting up stalactites and granite slabs with moss and algae as Ruthie plodded behind him. They wound through the passageway, rounding a couple of curves without seeing a brook. After twenty minutes, Moose hunched over.

"Swing the flashlight more to the left," Ruthie said. Had she imagined the creek?

Chapter Ten

Moose moved the flashlight from the ceiling of the cave to the bottom of it, beams of light dancing around the stalactites and stalagmites.

"There it is. There it is." Ruthie jumped up and down. "Look, there are the fish. Do you have a fishing pole in that football bag?"

Moose let out a half laugh. "No. But I have a pair of scissors." He raised his brows. "One of us could snag a fish with them."

By one of us, he meant her. "I guess we could try." Ruthie wasn't ready to accept a fisherwoman designation, especially if she had to catch a fish with a pair of scissors. But a vision of a fish sizzling in a pan flashed in her head. Maybe she could convince Moose to do it.

They practically ran to the front of the cave. Moose charged to his gear, pulled out the scissors and a small plastic bag. "Here." He handed them to Ruthie.

He'd just as well have asked her to take a ball of fire. "I thought you wanted to do it." Only a short while ago she had convinced herself she could contribute more. But stab a fish with a pair of scissors? If she didn't do it, they would eat cereal for dinner. She craved the fish for herself—and Moose. He needed a substantial meal. "I'll snag dinner."

"Yes." Moose gave her a thumbs up.

Ruthie grasped the scissors, holding them downward as they hurried to the stream. Surely, she could spear one. The poor little fishes couldn't even see. The technique probably required the skill of a dart thrower. She'd never thrown one, but it didn't matter. She was starving.

"All right, I sew a little, but I've only used these to cut fabric and thread. I've never punched anyone or anything with them."

"Think of the fish as a decoration you're sewing. You need to poke a big needle into it."

"Excellent suggestion." When faced with actually killing a living being, even though Ruthie's mouth watered at the thought of eating a scrumptious entrée, she hesitated. She ate fish, beef, and poultry, but she didn't pluck them from their natural habitat. Cereal could never replace a fish now that she'd seen one though. She loved mountain trout. She'd never seen a mountain trout swimming and these might not be trout, but they would do fine.

Moose peered at her with expectant eyes.

Ruthie got on her knees, holding the scissors high, ready to stab one of the unassuming fish. One swam by, but she couldn't do it. She hated to disappoint Moose, and she wanted the fish. She resumed her strike position.

A lone fish flipped its tail close to the bank. "Yes."

She lifted her weapon, followed through, and struck dirt. She let out a heavy sigh. "I'll do it."

"I know you will." Doubt lined Moose's voice.

The fish or starvation? Sorry little fishy. Trying to find the courage of a warrior, she imagined herself Napoleon in a fierce battle. An entire school approached. She zeroed in on her target, thrusting her arm high. "Ha-ya." She swooped down with a force she didn't realize was in her—and missed. The other fishes scattered. Ruthie sank down beside the water. Perhaps she had met her Waterloo.

"Try again—please."

Her stomach touched her backbone. It was just a fish. They didn't live very long anyway.

Moose leaned forward, eyeing the stream with intensity. "Here they come."

"Okay." She moved closer to the stream, knelt, and aimed her weapon above a fish, its tail swishing. The fish was too fast. Tears welled up and threatened to spill over her eyelashes, but she blinked them away. Next time.

"Here they come," Moose said.

She visualized the scissors held high, then moving downward, jabbing her prey. Imitating the action, she struck and speared one. "I got it. I got it. I got it." Ruthie held out her wriggling prize, a girlish laugh bubbling from her.

"Yes. Good job. Now get another one."

Ruthie's heart sank. "You're kidding."

"No, look. Here comes one. Go ahead. Add it to the fish you're holding."

Ruthie glanced at the fish trying to wiggle off of the scissor blade. Poor thing. She wasn't a hunter or fisher. A knot formed in her stomach. Yet, her concern for the fish couldn't satisfy her hunger. Sorry, little fish.

"Spear it now."

"Ha-ya." Done. Moose probably would never understand the toll killing the fishes had taken on her.

He opened the bag. "Put them here."

In the blink of an eye, she shoved the poor little fishes, scissors and all, into the bag. She couldn't stand to look at them.

Moose removed the weapon and closed the sack. "Hurry. Let's go eat." He skipped. "Hot diggity."

Seeing Moose's excitement trumped Ruthie's angst. She couldn't resist giving him a high-five. As they walked to the campsite, Ruthie stared at the fishes. She could hardly believe they were real.

Moose sat down with his back against the wall of the cave, stretched out, and took a fish out of the bag. Cleaning it with his pocket knife, he seemed content.

Even though hunger pangs plagued Ruthie, watching the process turned her stomach. Would she be able to eat the fish? "Eww, I can't look."

"I learned to clean fish at an early age. If you'd rather not witness my expertise, find something to use as a pan or roasting prong."

"If I can't find something, as famished as I am, I might hold my portion over the flame."

"You'll have to look at it if you do."

Moose's playfulness must've sprung from his anticipation of dinner. Joy bubbled inside Ruthie because she had done something for him, even if killing the poor little fishes had been difficult. "I could manage if I set my mind to it."

"I bet you could."

Ruthie rummaged in Moose's football gear until she remembered a purchase she'd made. She unzipped her bag and waved frantically. "I may have something." She threw items from her luggage. "If only they're here." She mumbled. "Yes." She couldn't stop a big grin as she held up two mini pecan pies in tin foil pans. "Look. I purchased these at the gas station before I left the campus."

Moose's eyes grew as wide as the tins. "Wonderful. We can eat them for dessert, right?"

"Yes." Ruthie pried the sweet goodies from their containers and placed them on the two napkins that came with them.

Moose put each of the fish in one of the pans. Making a small fire, he let it die to nearly embers. "We couldn't have asked for a better entrée. Fish cook easily and a hamburger would take forever over a fire no bigger than this."

"I've never helped prepare a meal that smells as good as this one." This small fish blessed them richly, but she'd make sure Moose had a hamburger in his future.

He said grace, then used a T-shirt as a hot pad and set Ruthie's fish in front of her. He directed his gaze to his dish, flipped the T-shirt in the air, and laughed. "Oh, yeah."

Ruthie gulped down her fish in no time, then handed Moose dessert. "Here ya' go."

"If we had a TV airing a good football game, I'd be right at home." Moose laughed.

"Yes, and you could explain it all to me." Ruthie ate her treat. Afterward her eyelids grew heavy, so she lay down on the blanket. The last thing she remembered before she fell asleep—Moose pulling the coverlet over her.

She awoke, springing upward at the sound of a loud bang. Moose yanked on his coat as she tugged on hers, her gloves, and the knit hat Moose had loaned her. He tossed her a flashlight before he yanked their clothes from the faux clothesline and scooped up the bags. "Get the thermoses and get out of here." They ran to the other end of the cave and charged into the woods, slipping and sliding on the ice.

Crack, crack, thud.

"Turn off the flashlight and run as fast as you can."

"It's pitch dark out here."

"There's a little moonlight. Our sight will adjust."

Was he crazy? Racing in the black of night was as dangerous as Hucklesford. "We have to see where we're going."

"You're right. Turn on the flashlight. Cup your hand over it."

Pounding the ground, Ruthie broke up the ice. Pellets hit her cheeks. "Why doesn't he go away? Where are we going?"

"I don't know. If you saw a cabin to the right, we'll stay on course toward it. Pray we find it." Moose looked down. "How's your ankle?"

"I can speed up if I have to." Her injury ached, but the drive to stay alive outweighed the pain.

Crack, crack, crack, thud.

Ruthie jumped a foot off of the ground and staggered.

Moose grasped her arm before she fell. "I can tell by the sound of his shots he's farther away from us now."

A fire burned inside Ruthie to find safety. Peering as far as she could see amid the cloud cover, she checked the area to their right, then the left. She repeated the action again and again. Nothing but leafless trees. Could they escape Hucklesford, or find a good place to hide before he caught them?

Chapter Eleven

Moose listened for more shots as the sun rising sent a glow over his and Ruthie's path. Hearing none, he slowed their pace.

Ruthie hobbled, obviously struggling on her hurt ankle. Guilt hit him like a two by four for suggesting they stay at the cabin. Yet, what could he have done differently? Left her in a car about to roll over a cliff? Hardly.

It had seemed so simple to take her to a deserted pioneer home, where they could rest in comfort, then return to the highway to find help. He never imagined they'd end up in a wilderness void of humanity except for one person trying to kill them.

He'd never wanted to protect anyone as much as he did Ruthie. He wasn't sure why. Maybe it stemmed from self-reproach over the disaster his well-intended trek to find shelter had turned into. Whatever it was, it consumed him. He pulled out his cell phone and turned it on.

Ruthie's eyes snapped wide. "Yes?"

"Sorry." He'd as soon try to land in a safe spot from the eye of a hurricane as to navigate through this frigid no-man's-land. Thank goodness, playing football had taught him to keep getting up after someone knocked him down. And coaching, well, he already missed his players. When one of them sprained an ankle, after the trainer taped it, he returned to action, jogging onto the field.

Ruthie didn't play football. She didn't have access to the therapies the team doctor used to make the players' wounds heal quicker either. Seeing her lips turned down and her dull eyes with no sparkle cut into his heart. "Maybe we can rest. I haven't heard a gunshot recently."

Ruthie wrung her hands, the thermoses bashing together. "It's snowing pretty hard again. Am I making tracks?"

"I don't think so." Moose looked at his feet. "My boots have patterns on the soles, but unless this creep's a professional tracker, I don't think he can follow the faint prints we're leaving." Ruthie looked so fragile. "The shoes I loaned you have cleats, but you need them. We can't have you stumbling anymore."

"Those gun blasts really frightened me. Could we go back to see if we made prints in the snow?"

Moose opened his mouth to say no.

She looked at him with wide, intense eyes.

A quiver hit his stomach. "We need to put as much distance between us and Hucklesford as we can."

"I know."

He let out a loud sigh. "Okay. Just a few feet."

They walked by a squirrel eating while perched on his hind legs. Moose pointed at the furry little animal as it flipped its tail and scampered off. "How he found a nut in all of this snow and ice I'll never know. I guess he remembers where he stored food for the winter." He gazed about, searching for signs of other animals. "Look, there's a catamount on a ledge in the distance. He's probably roamed around down here. I don't believe anyone would think these spotty impressions on the ice belong to a big cat. They surely couldn't tell if a human made them."

Ruthie eyed the marks. "You're right. I'm sorry I delayed us."

"No problem. Let's locate that house."

"Since we haven't seen it, I wonder if I made it up. You know, the way people in a desert think they see an oasis where there isn't one."

Moose swung his hand in the air to dismiss Ruthie's words. "I doubt you did any such thing. You're much too intelligent and realistic for that."

~

Ruthie's self-confidence rose after Moose's praise. Odd, if she met Moose at a college function, she wouldn't say much to him because they shared nothing in common. Yet, he'd done more for her perception of men than any of the few guys she dated in high school or college. She peered up at him.

"What?"

Ruthie put her hand on her neck as heat rushed up it. She didn't want to profess how much she admired him. After all, she expected to lose contact with him after the two of them returned to Hilltop. "I, uh…"

Moose broke eye contact. "We're lost, and it's my fault."

"No, it isn't. You've kept us safe under horrible conditions. We even rested in a warm, dry place last night. As you mentioned, if we'd had a television, it would've been just like home."

Moose's deep-barreled laugh filled the air. "You are too much."

Why had he said that? She meant every word. She meant them because…because Moose was with her. That turned the cave into a home.

"I suppose I'm aggravated I can't find the house you saw. We're roughing it for the fourth day. I've never played in or coached a football game as challenging as this jaunt to nowhere. It has to end."

That's what jarred Ruthie's insides each morning she awoke in these backwoods—the possibility their journey would never end—at least not in a good way. "Yeah, I can't give enough thanks for running water and electricity. At least no one has fired at us lately."

Moose raised his arm in the victory sign. "I see the house."

Ruthie jumped up and down, the thermos bottles banging into the silence. "I'm not hallucinating. There is a house."

Moose pointed to the right. "It's on top of that peak. That's probably why you glimpsed it when you took your tumble."

"I can't believe we found it." She took hold of Moose's arm. "It's quite a few miles from here. How long will it take us to reach it?"

"It's hard to say."

"Just so we get there before Hucklesford fires at us again." Ruthie raised a thermos. "Onward. I can't imagine why anyone would live in such a remote area, but I'm glad someone does."

Remote. Ruthie was part of a neighborhood. Yet, she isolated herself from others. In Florida, she had socialized with an affluent crowd to fill a void in her life. They were like cotton candy—all fluff and no substance. She couldn't wait to get out of these backwoods. She'd make friends, maybe host a luncheon. Oh, but how she would miss Moose when they parted ways.

When they finally reached a clearing, Moose pulled the waterproof blanket out of his bag and spread it on a big rock. "Let's have lunch, cereal, and a protein drink. While we eat, we'll plan the most secure course we can."

They plopped down and assembled their meal.

Ruthie munched the cereal. It tasted like cardboard, but it kept her from starving. She couldn't agree more with Moose about finding safe passage. "Walking in the open with nowhere to hide frightens me. If only I could convince myself the last shot had come from a hunter, I'd do it. I know better though." She gulped down the protein drink.

Moose turned up his thermos and sipped. "We are smack in the middle of a patch of land with no trees or foliage. It'll take longer to walk around the edge of this barren plot, but if we cross it, we have no cover."

"As much as I want to get to the house, I'd rather not make myself a target."

"Then it's settled." Moose raked his hand in his cereal box as though he searched for another bite. He sighed. "I'm finished with lunch. How about you?"

Ruthie took the last bite of her cereal and swallowed. "Yep."

Moose gathered the litter, stuffed it into a small plastic container, and put it in his duffle bag. "Change the dressing on your wounds and we'll leave."

Ruthie did as Moose asked, then pulled her cell phone from her purse and turned it on. Moose raised his eyebrows and gave her a questioning look.

"No." A cell phone signal was something she remembered from another life.

"I figured as much." Moose picked up the bags. "Let's go."

By the time the sun lay low in the sky, they reached the base of the steep peak they needed to climb.

Moose gazed at the incline. "We can't make it to the top before dark. Let's find a place near here."

Ruthie relaxed her tense muscles as thankfulness for rest filled her.

"If we start early in the morning, we should arrive sometime tomorrow."

"Sounds good." She followed Moose out of the dell and scanned the area. Other than a few evergreens, only solid white earth and hardwood trees lay before her." "Is this it?""

"I'll look around for something better while we still have twilight." Moose put down the bags and left.

Ruthie pulled out the rainproof blanket and sat on it amid the early evening fog. The frigid air tightened her skin. Even with the down coat, the cold sent an ache all the way to her bones. She lay down and pulled the blanket around her for extra warmth. Exhausted, she fell asleep until loud high-pitched barking jerked her awake. Flinging off her covering, she sat straight up. A coyote howled only ten feet from her.

Chapter Twelve

Ruthie shook, breaking up the icy earth where she sat next to a hardwood tree. *Don't move.* She held her breath and tried to think.

The reddish-brown coyote must've smelled her fear. Like an angry dog, it bared its teeth, then rocked on all fours.

Ruthie inhaled.

The coyote reared backward, and yowled.

Ruthie scrunched up.

The predator sprang forward, barking. Its teeth morphed into rows of saws. Then, the trees in front of her in the distance spun.

The coyote lunged a foot.

Ruthie's heart beat like a jackhammer. She had to do something. Moose's bag lay right beside her. Get a flashlight. She inched her fingers forward. Closer…closer…closer…

A yowl pierced her ears.

Ruthie froze, then barely wiggled her hand.

The attacker's lips curled over its teeth.

Her fingertips brushed the end of a flashlight.

The monster's mouth opened like a bear trap. A

deep growl rattled in its throat, its eyes wild, boring a hole through Ruthie.

The barking faded. Slipping, slipping away, Ruthie drifted. *I must stay conscious.*

The animal jerked another foot forward.

Ruthie snatched the flashlight. Switched it on and swung it back and forth.

The light hit the coyote's face. The beast quieted, turning its head away from Ruthie as Moose approached them.

A weight lifted from Ruthie's shoulders.

Moose shined his flashlight on the coyote.

It turned toward him.

Ruthie swirled her flashlight, flooding the coyote with bright beams.

Moose threw sticks at it.

The angry animal scurried away, yelping.

Ruthie collapsed on Moose's chest.

He held her tight. "We won't stay here. Pack up. Each day I'm sorrier than the day before I got us into this mess. Each day I think the ice will thaw, or the phones will work." Moose's expression closed down.

Ruthie gave him a hug. "It isn't your fault. You were trying to help. There's no telling what's happened on the highway. We might have gone over the cliff with our cars if we'd stayed in them. If it weren't for you, I may have frozen to death on the highway, or in this forest."

Moose's expression turned as soft as satin as he released her. "I'm glad I met you, but I sure wish our circumstances were different."

Ruthie flung her arms around Moose's neck. He ran his finger down her cheek and his lips met hers. The white forest disappeared, and Ruthie's world stood still in a land of flowers and rainbows. When Moose released her, he said, "I promise I'm going to get us out of here."

Ruthie hopped up. "And after you do, I'm coming to your house to watch football." She couldn't bear the thought of not spending time with Moose ever again. After all, he had sealed his invitation with a kiss. Ruthie directed her gaze to the side. She still wondered if he'd forget about her when they returned to campus. She could see how these woods could do strange things to a person, like make an outgoing, athletic football coach think he was attracted to a solitary advanced grammar professor who parsed nouns for a living.

"Yes, you are."

Every nerve wound tight by danger and fear of freezing relaxed, while Ruthie floated away with Moose. They trudged deeper into the woods, winding around leafless, icy trees until they found a spot underneath an enormous boulder surrounded by snow-white hardwoods.

"I like this much better," Moose said as he set down the bags. "I'll gather firewood." He gave Ruthie a quick hug, then darted into the forest.

She dropped the thermos bottles. "Wait for me. I'd rather not stay here with the coyotes."

"Okay."

Ruthie joined him, and they walked a quarter of a mile with the flashlight cutting into nothing but foggy darkness before he finally spotted a large limb. He hoisted it and turned toward their campsite. As Ruthie walked beside him, she picked up twigs.

When they reached their belongings, Moose

studied his prize. "I need an ax, but I'll turn this into logs somehow." He dropped the heavy limb, then walked around, swinging his arms back and forth. "Loosening my muscles."

"I can see why. That piece of firewood's pretty thick. How are we going to chop it?"

"We won't. We'll start the fire with kindling. Then I'll extend part of the limb over the flame while the fire burns through the wood farther down." Moose knelt, put his hand on the log, and turned it over several times. Then he straightened. "I'll burn through it twice and create three logs."

"You'll catch on fire."

"No, I'll be careful."

Ruthie twisted a button on her coat. "It's awfully risky." She sized up their potential for burning through the wood safely. "We'll each hold one end."

"That thing's heavy."

Ruthie bent over and touched a thin area. "Let's start here."

He gave her a wink. "Are you sure there are no backwoods pioneer women in your ancestry?"

Ruthie giggled. "As far as I know, I come from a long line of English teachers, but every family closet has secrets."

Moose let out a chuckling puff of air. "So they do." He piled up twigs for kindling, then Ruthie added several small branches. After Moose lit the fire, he positioned the large tree limb over the blaze. Ruthie held the slighter portion while vibrant reddish-orange flames licked the log like finely shaped tongues. The strong branch held its own though.

Ruthie's arms ached and shook. Trying to see how

far the brilliant-colored fire wrapped around the wood, she leaned forward. The bit of black showing encouraged her. She would not drop her part of the limb now. She tightened her grasp.

Moose eyed her. "I can grab this thing on either side of the flames and break it the rest of the way."

Ruthie huffed. "I'm fine. Look. It's about to go any second. When it comes apart, both ends will fall."

"No. Let go."

The flames sucked up the last piece of timber in the middle of the large branch. Ruthie hopped out of the way as her portion fell, sparks of fire flashing.

Moose moved backward and dropped his end of the log away from the fire. Afterward, he used a leftover piece of kindling to push Ruthie's portion farther into the flames. When the blaze caught the wood and swooshed upward, Moose motioned toward it. "Warmth."

They stood in front of the fire for several minutes, then Moose pulled a blanket from his football bag and spread it on the boulder. After he lay on it, he placed his hands behind his head and directed his gaze toward Ruthie. "Come here."

Ruthie lay down beside him and rested her head on his chest, which seemed soft compared to what she'd slept on the past two nights. A few short days ago, spending time with a man was as far from Ruthie's world as Mars. Lying next to a football coach in the middle of a frozen forest seemed surreal. "We need to burn through the timber one more time."

"Yep, but let's relax while it cools, have cereal and protein drinks, maybe."

Before Ruthie could answer, she fell asleep.

An hour later, she woke up.

After they ate cereal and drank protein drinks, Moose poured water over the charred end of the large limb he'd put aside to make sure it was cool. Then he and Ruthie held it over the fire until they had two more logs.

Moose brushed off his hands. "That's it. We're in good shape for the rest of the night. We'll stay warm while the fire scares away unfriendly creatures. Make yourself as comfortable as possible and get some sleep. We have a mountain to scale in the morning."

Ruthie questioned what lay before them. Scenarios about the resident of the house atop the hill swirled in her brain. Who would greet them? A friend? Or a foe?

~

Moose stayed awake plotting a course for tomorrow. He would walk in strange territory. When he and Dad had gone hunting, they had always stayed around the cabin.

Dad. Other than his size, he shared nothing with him. As a youngster, he'd tried to please Dad and win his love. Still, their relationship remained like parallel streets, running side by side, but never meeting.

Thank goodness for Mom. She'd supported his desire to play football while demanding he remember his athletic ability was a gift from God. He'd made her words his goal. He peeked at Ruthie. This night, he had only one goal. Get Ruthie to safety.

Chapter Thirteen

Moose awoke as morning broke, the sun shielded by heavy fog. He hopped up and struck matches underneath low hanging icicles, placing the thermos bottles below them. After he filled the containers with dripping water, he added protein powder. "Here." He offered one to Ruthie. "Drink this before we clean up our litter and start our trek to the house."

"Thank you." She gulped it. "I can't wait to get there."

Moose held up his hand in stop fashion. "I see someone walking among the trees in the distance."

Ruthie put her hand over her mouth. "It's him. There's no one else out here. Can he see us?"

"I don't think so. It's so foggy. We need to get out of here though."

They snatched up their belongings and continued up the hill.

"It's eerie knowing he's out there, but we can't see him or hear him. I'm itching all over to know where he is."

Twigs broke behind Ruthie, and she jumped.

Moose put his arm around her. "Keep going," he whispered.

"This is the most frightened I've been. We don't know where he is. It's like I'm in a war in a foxhole waiting for the enemy to appear out of the fog and kill me."

"Shhh. Just keep walking. We're fine."

Another twig broke behind them.

"But I know he's out there."

Halfway up the mountainside, Moose stopped and spoke softly. "Uh-oh, I'm not sure if we can walk on this, but we can throw him off here."

"What's wrong with it?" Ruthie whispered.

"It's a scree slope. Some hikers think they're fun to climb. Unfortunately, it contains loose rocks. A misstep can send the pebbles spiraling, creating a tumble all the way to the bottom—not a cushy ride."

"It sounds dangerous."

"We simply need to step on the top of it though." He tapped his foot. "I imagine the weather's turned everything into a solid chunk of ice. Let's see." He bent down and pushed on the frozen rocks with his gloved hand. "It appears steady."

Ruthie eyed the formation. "I see the problem. If one stone breaks loose, it disturbs another one, so on and so forth."

"Yes, English teacher, then we go so on and so forth rolling down the hill." He rubbed his foot in a circle over the scree slope. "If we take this route, we might lose Hucklesford. Let me try. If it holds me, we know it won't collapse with you."

Ruthie picked at her fingernail. "Even with ice covering them, the frozen rocks and sticks could cause a bruise. Landing on one with a sharp point could jab or cut a person."

"You're right, but surely with the bitter weather day after day, they're frozen solid. We can't stand around forever debating the matter." Moose moved to the top of the scree. "I'm going to test it." Holding one bag on either side of him to balance his weight, he took a stride with his left foot, then slowly brought up his right. Encouraged by the rocks staying in place, he advanced until he stood only three feet from the other side.

Uh-oh. In his determination to walk on the scree, he'd left Ruthie to attempt the dangerous excursion alone. His left foot slid and his chest tightened. Two pebbles broke loose, then an avalanche of stones knocking against each other fell beneath him. He dropped the bags to clutch the edge of the slope, but his hands slid past it.

Glimpsing the landscape as fast as he could, he looked for something to hold on to as Ruthie's screams filled the air.

Shots rang out.

Moose's stomach roiled as though scree nuggets rolled around in it. More of the slope gave way. A piece of rubble hit him on the top of his head. Out of the corner of his right eye, he glimpsed a tree trunk. Reaching as far as he could stretch with all his might, he grasped—air.

Bang. Bang.

Moose's feet collided with fragments underneath him. He clawed at the rocks as more of the hill broke loose until he grabbed at a limb on a small tree growing out of the scree—air again. Black spots danced in his eyes. Like an out-of-sync acrobat, he tumbled. He flung out his hands, touched a branch, and tightened his grip. Finally, the world stilled.

Bang. Bang. Bang.

Where was Ruthie? He lifted his gaze. Thank goodness she was safe. The only thing, she sat sobbing. He was halfway between her and the bottom of the scree. "I'm alright."

Bang. Bang. Bang. Bang.

"Try to find cover."

"I'm coming," Ruthie's sweet voice drifted to him.

"Nooooo."

Ruthie sniffled. "You're hurt."

"No, I'm okay. I'm going to make my way to the bottom of the scree. If you'll get somewhere safe, I'll come back and get you." Hopefully, she would do as he asked.

"No. I'm coming to you," Ruthie called out.

Bang. Bang. Bang. Bang.

Ruthie screamed. "Where are the shots coming from."

"Above us. You'll be alright as long as he can't see you. I doubt he can see either of us in the thick fog."

"He knows we're here."

Moose tensed up and pain shot through his ribcage.

Bang. Bang. Bang. Bang.

Hucklesford would run out of bullets soon. If only he and Ruthie could get off of this scree.

He listened for Ruthie. Why didn't she say something? Did Hucklesford shoot her? *Oh, please, Lord, no.* "Have you started down yet?"

"Yes."

They had to get off of this scree. "You're not in my line of sight. Are you holding onto sturdy boughs?"

"Yes."

Several small sticks and loose pebbles rolled by. Moose jumped and nearly let go of the tree. Trying to see Ruthie again, he stretched his entire body to the left. "Hucklesford must be re-loading. Where are you?"

"I'm coming toward you." Sadness rang in her voice.

Thank goodness, he didn't hear her crying. In spite of his insides racing, he attempted to stay calm. "Can you describe your position?"

"I'm three feet from the slide, ten feet above you."

Moose directed his gaze toward Ruthie's voice and his hand slipped. More nuggets and sticks fell. He shivered all over. "What's going on? Where's all the debris coming from?"

"Some twigs and limbs fell off of the trees when the stones broke. I think Hucklesford shot some of them loose."

He'd made a big mistake. *Please, Lord, give me a second chance to get Ruthie to safety.* A sensation he couldn't explain washed over him. Confidence he and Ruthie would get to the house filled him.

He surveyed the landscape to his left. Twelve inches from him, a piece of granite protruded from the steep grade. How did he get to it? He broke out in a cold sweat. "Ruthie, stay where you are until I call you. I'm going to maneuver onto your path."

"Wait until I get there. I'll help."

"Nooo." Moose's nerves grated like misaligned car gears. That woman was impossible. Could she not understand he had enough to deal with?

"I can at least hold on to you to help you balance."

"That's the craziest idea I've heard lately."

"Really? I'm not the one who stepped on the scree slope." Crying wafted down the slope.

Now he'd done it. "Stay where you are." Every hair on Moose's arm stood on end. "Don't take another step, or I'll let go of this tree."

More weeping resounded from above. "I could show you how to place your feet on a safe spot while he's not firing. I have a better vantage point."

If she would only take care of herself and leave him to do the same. She was right about her vantage point. She was always right about something. That irritated him as much as the snow on his eyelashes partially blocking his vision. "Okay, I'll tell you what. As long as you stay where you are until I'm situated, you can help. How far are you above me now?"

"Four feet at most."

"Good. You mentioned something I could stand on, right?"

"Yes, close to you, there's a slab of granite that looks like a step."

"I saw it. Is there anything nearby I could grasp before I let go of this tree?"

"Stretch your left leg to the left. It will touch the granite. You can wrap your right arm around the trunk of a small tree twelve inches above the slab. You should clutch the tree with your right arm and step to the left."

Moose pondered Ruthie's words, then peered up. He tried to see around the trunk of the tree he held onto—impossible.

"I'll pray."

"I will too. Count on it." He shifted his weight as far as he could to the left without letting go of the young oak he held onto. His foot swung in the air.

A shot rang out.

Gravel below him broke loose. He tightened his grip and pulled back his foot, spraining his ankle. Fighting dizziness, he gritted his teeth.

"Are you alright?"

Moose asked, "Where did I go wrong?"

"Don't take such a big step. Edge your foot to the left a little at a time."

He said another prayer. Without looking down, he visualized his foot landing on the step-like granite. He still couldn't see the tree Ruthie mentioned, but he trusted her. He edged his foot to the left as he stepped into thin air.

Shots whizzed above him.

His heart clenched. He quickly withdrew his foot. "Are you okay?"

"Yes, I'm fine. We need to get you off of this thing."

From watching his players move on the field advance inches at a time in close plays, Moose sensed how much distance he needed to cover.

Debris fell past him.

His stomach churned like a washing machine as he inched his foot over and shoved his right arm up.

Grabbed the tree.

Muscle spasms wracked his biceps. His feet dangled.

He could see Ruthie hanging onto a tree across from him.

He edged his left leg into thin air. His pulse beat in

his temples.

His right leg swung in the breeze.

"The bottom's close. Bring your left foot down a little at a time. It will hit the protruding granite." Ruthie's voice quivered.

Hoping his foot landed on something solid, he inched it lower.

"There's the ledge."

Moose's hands grew clammy. It took all the guts he had left, but he eased his foot to the piece of granite, reached up with his right arm and let go of the small tree he had held onto.

Shots blasted, hitting the back of the protruding granite, barely missing his foot.

He jumped and slid. Dug his fingernails into the ice. They didn't stick. The world around him spun as he rolled down the slope, sliding past some stones, banging against others.

Ruthie screamed and reached out to grab him as he plummeted toward the bottom of the scree.

He bounced off a large chunk of ice and hit a tree.

Chapter Fourteen

Moose groaned. Mom's dog smooched him. "Bruiser, go away."

"What?"

Moose raised his eyelids at the sound of Ruthie's sweet voice. A gray sky over him. The harshness of winter around him. And then—Ruthie came into view. She bent over him, pecking his cheeks with tender kisses.

"Please wake up. Please wake up."

Moose flinched to think he'd mistaken Ruthie for Bruiser. He reached up and wiped her tears. "I'm alright. I can't believe I fell, and Hucklesford, where's he?"

"I don't know. After you tumbled to the bottom of the scree, the gunshots stopped. Maybe he thought…"

"Thought I killed myself?"

"I wasn't going to say that." Ruthie hugged him. "I'm so glad you're okay, but we have to make sure nothing's broken."

Moose tried to raise up, to tell her not to worry. Moving his noggin' hurt. He touched it. "Ouch."

Ruthie wiped her tears. "Move your arms and

legs."

He did as she asked. "No problem. They're fine, except for the ankle, but I strained a rib muscle on my first fall."

"You...you... were unconscious." Crying, Ruthie spluttered her words.

"Shhh. No. No. I hit the tree on my side. It knocked the wind out of me, but I'm fine now." Moose placed his hand on top of Ruthie's. "I have a little knot on my head where a rock hit me." He rubbed his gloved hand over the icy earth. "I won't have any trouble finding ice to put on it." He uttered a soft, half-baked chuckle.

Ruthie kept a staid expression as she hopped up. "I'll get some now."

"Stop. It isn't necessary." Moose's words fell into thin air as Ruthie charged to a large rock with lots of icicles hanging off of it.

She snapped off several, hurried to Moose, snatched off his toboggan, and applied the treatment. "Here?"

"Over a little, kind of at the crown." When he took her hand to move it to the knot, a sweet sensation sent tingles across his skin. For a moment, the pain went away. "That's good, thank you," he said as though nothing had happened while he wanted to hold Ruthie and kiss her passionately. He wouldn't though. He couldn't risk a distraction with danger lurking around the corner.

Ruthie threw down the remainder of the ice. "Let's find a place in the woods and rest until tomorrow."

Moose sighed. They needed to get away from here before Hucklesford shot at them again. How much more could one tiny grammar professor endure? The way her shoulders slumped, he concluded she needed a break as much, or more than he did. Yet, Moose suspected Hucklesford lurked, waiting for the right moment to shoot at them again.

Ruthie dried Moose's hair with a T-shirt from his bag and placed his knit hat on his head. Spotting his gloves nearby, she retrieved them.

"Thank you. If you aren't too tired, we can search for the house. Maybe we can reach it sometime tonight."

"Can you even walk?"

Moose tried to push up. Pain ran through his rib muscle. He hoped Ruthie didn't notice how uncomfortable he was. She had enough to contend with without him adding to her load. He attempted to get up again, but each movement brought sharp, piercing agony. "I have an idea. I'll show you how to tape my rib. Then I'll take care of my ankle."

Ruthie looked up. "Why didn't I think of that?"

Moose forced what he hoped turned out as a grin and did his best to keep the strain from his fall out of his voice. "You're not a coach. We're familiar with sprains and bruises and how to treat them."

Ruthie dug through the football gear.

Moose hated to ask her to tape his chest. After all, she wasn't a nurse. He couldn't imagine her interests lay in medicine with a degree in advanced grammar. If he intended to carry the bags, he had no choice if he wanted to avoid extra stress on the injury. "Look for strips in a plastic baggie labeled for the rib muscle. We'll need three."

She pulled out the dressings.

Moose removed his coat and heavy sweatshirt. Anxiety over whether Ruthie could apply the bandages correctly before Hucklesford shot at them again created goosebumps. He didn't want her to know that though. "It's cold without clothing." He pointed to a spot on his ribcage, then held up a bandage. "Without applying pressure, stick this here." He pointed to an area above the pulled muscle. "Repeat the procedure just below the injured spot." As she taped the ends on the second strip, he let out a sigh of relief. Two down.

Ruthie jerked her hand away. "Are you alright? Did I hurt you?"

"No. You did a great job. Thank you." Inside he hollered in pain, but he refused to let the sound escape. "We're ready for the last strip." He gave her another bandage. "Peel off the paper slips and apply the tape directly to the injured muscle."

Ruthie did as Moose asked and quickly pulled his sweatshirt over his head.

Satisfied he could deal with the luggage, his tight muscles unwound, including the one in his ribcage. Ruthie was much better at the task than he had imagined. Apparently, she was a quick study for lots of things—climbing, camping, spearing fish. He put on his jacket, then took care of his ankle.

~

Ruthie watched Moose as he took his first few steps. He hobbled a bit, but seemed okay. He didn't need to carry a heavy load though. "Let me take one bag."

"No. I'm fine."

"I should take one. Honestly, I have nothing but my purse and the thermoses. I'll swap them for a bag."

"You have a wounded leg."

"It's much better." Ruthie reached over and yanked at a duffle bag. "Give it here."

"Ouch. Stop it."

Ruthie pulled at it again. What a stubborn man. If he didn't give her a bag, she was going to explode from frustration. From the way his body sagged on the injured side, she guessed the weight bothered him. She sent him her sternest teacher look.

"Whew! You must be a terror in the classroom." He took out one small piece of luggage and handed it to her. "This one is lighter. You can carry it for a while, but return it when you get tired."

"It won't add more physical stress." That was impossible. She was already exhausted. As they passed the last of the fallen debris at the bottom of the slope, Ruthie tried to put the horror the scree and Hucklesford had caused behind her. She yearned to continue until they found the house.

They embarked on a slick trail near the scree leading back to the top of the hill. Trees with low-hanging boughs they could hold on to made the trek easier. When they approached a large boulder jutting out of the side of an incline, Moose halted. "What a find. We can sit under here and eat. Then, if we decide to stay, we can make ourselves fairly comfortable."

After they dropped the bags, Ruthie spread out a blanket while Moose concocted their protein drinks. She'd wondered how much more protein powder and cereal he had, but she couldn't bring herself to ask. Did she really want to know?

They sat down on a small ledge underneath the granite overhang, then Moose served their meal—such as it was.

Ruthie listened for the animals and Hucklesford, but nothing disturbed the silent snow. She imagined the frozen ground in the valley bursting into spring. How beautiful—a floor of green grass. She imagined plush trees with proud, green leaves showing off their blossoms of purple, white, and pink lining the hollow at the edge of the forest. Basking in her imaginary world, she glimpsed a shadow.

She leaned forward to get a better look, but a thick fog passed in her field of vision. She rose and strained to see through the low-lying mist. Finally, the film dissipated, the sun glinting on the ice below, exposing someone meandering around the bottom of the scree. Who else? With her solace fading like the day's light, she pointed with a shaky finger. "Is that Hucklesford?"

Moose sprang up. "I think so. It looks as though he's trying to figure out where we are."

Ruthie snatched the thermoses, one bag, and her purse and hurried up the incline. "If it's Hucklesford, how long will it take him to catch us?"

"My guess—he doesn't know if we took the right or left side of the hill. We'll finish hiking up the left as fast as we can and hope he chooses the right."

"Can he see us?"

"I don't know, but he's only twenty feet below, and we saw *him*. We'll know soon enough."

Chapter Fifteen

Ruthie's protein drink churned in her stomach as she followed Moose past the hardwoods and pines covered in ice and snow.

Moose stared at the hill. "Since the path on the other side of the scree looks like an easier climb, Hucklesford will probably think we took it."

Ruthie adjusted the warm knit hat Moose had loaned her. "We need to go as fast as possible, but we can't fall. You should take it easy on the ankle too. How is it?"

"It's alright, but yes, steady does it. Thank goodness, holding onto the tree limbs will allow both of us to take weight off of our injuries. We've trudged up steeper grades." Moose winked at Ruthie. "We'll make short-order of this."

Not long after nightfall, they emerged at the top of the ridge. Exhausted, Ruthie sat on the hard, cold earth. "I scaled this incline the fastest of any so far. I think we left Hucklesford way behind us, but I don't see the house. Should we try to find it and knock on the door tonight?" Ruthie pulled up her knees and grasped them.

"It makes no difference because the person who

lives in it is our only hope."

"You're right. If we locate it, and it's not too late, let's introduce ourselves."

They wandered about the wooded area for what seemed like hours, but was probably only forty-five minutes. Finally, they stopped to catch their breaths. Moose focused the light to the left—more frosty trees. To the right it shone on the same wintry landscape. Then he aimed it straight.

Ruthie gasped. Like a phoenix rising from ice instead of ashes, the house appeared. Nestled into a clearing among hardwoods and evergreen shrubs, it was a brick ranch with a concrete porch spanning the width of the home. "It really exists. It's like finding the pot of gold at the end of the rainbow."

"Who's out there?" A loud voice filled the air.

Ruthie stepped back several feet.

A porch light flicked on and a tall man with ebony skin and dreadlocks pointed a rifle at them. Ruthie leapt to Moose's side. Had they run from one criminal to another?

"Don't shoot. We're stranded." Moose's voice sounded calm under the circumstances.

"Stranded? From where? There's nothing out here."

Ruthie gripped Moose's arm.

"We wrecked our cars and nearly tumbled over the cliff on Highway 130 the day the ice storm hit." Moose shifted his weight.

Ruthie had never wanted to run from anywhere as much as she did from here. Her ears roared like a revved-up car engine. She couldn't stop focusing on the man's weapon. He couldn't have created more terror if he'd pointed a cannon at her. She wouldn't dare move, not even a twitch. What if he shot Moose, her, or both of them?

"I remembered a deserted cabin from visiting this area with my dad, so we went there to stay the night. It looked inhabited, and she..." Moose tilted his head toward Ruthie. "She recalled a news report about a criminal in this area. We hurried out of there, looking for safety. We mean no harm to you or anyone else."

The rifle wiggled. "No way, you serious about the criminal?"

Moose stood tall, as though he didn't fear the man. "Yes, I am. He killed three people in a jewelry store robbery."

"And you know this murderer came to the North Carolina Mountains?" The man sounded worried.

"Yes."

A moment of silence fell after Moose answered. Then the man said, "So, you left the cabin, took off through the woods, and wandered here."

Ruthie heard doubt in the man's tone. She clamped down harder on Moose's arm and forced words through her dry throat. "That's right. I fell on a steep incline and rolled to the bottom. On the way down, I glimpsed a home in the distance. That's why we hiked in this direction." Her voice quivered. Surely, he could see they needed help, but did he care, or worse yet, intend to harm them? The string of hope she had held onto since she saw the house broke.

Ruthie surveyed the landscape on the right, then the left, searching for a way to escape. Unfortunately, she didn't see one. "Could you put down that weapon? My friend..." Ruthie glanced at Moose... "doesn't carry one, and I certainly don't." She tried to sound authoritative, but her teacher's tone had left her. That was all right. She was lucky she'd found the wherewithal to say anything.

The man gripped the rifle. They'd journeyed all this way and found the barrel of an unsteady gun pointed at them. All she could do was hold on to Moose. Could he talk their way out of this?

"If you don't want to let us inside to warm up, that's fine. We'll go." Moose gave a quick nod toward Ruthie. "Ready?"

"More than." Ruthie rose on her tip-toes and whispered in Moose's ear. "Do you think he'll pull the trigger if we move?"

Moose snatched up his football bag. "I hope not."

Ruthi picked up the satchel, which might as well have weighed one hundred pounds the way the incident had sucked the strength out of her.

"Sit down. We're not finished yet."

Ruthie nearly fell down as the blood drained from her head. Then the glacial trees spun. She picked up a small, ice-covered stone and rubbed it over the nape of her neck. Moose plopped down beside her and took her hand. How many more hills could she climb? How much terror could she overcome?

"Who are you?" Anger lined the man's tone.

Ruthie opened her mouth, but could no longer force words out of it. She crumpled against Moose.

He introduced them and explained they were going home for Christmas vacation when they ended up in the storm. "Look, it's okay if you don't want us on your property. We gathered our belongings." Moose stood and pulled Ruthie up.

"I didn't say that." The guy spoke in a softer, calmer tone.

Moose and Ruthie glanced at each other, then at the man.

Had his attitude changed, or did he want them to stay to kill them? Shaking all over, Ruthie wished she'd never seen the house, and they'd never come here.

"Tell me a little more about yourselves." He aimed the weapon to the right away from them.

Ruthie took a sigh of relief.

Moose blurted out, "We're praying people. How about you?"

"Uh, uh, my parents took me to church. I'm a Christian."

Ruthie had her doubts about the man's faith. How could a Christian hold them at gunpoint, especially after they said they would leave?

"Then we have something in common," Moose said. "What else do you want to know about us? We need help, but the Lord will provide."

Yeah, we don't need yours, Ruthie wanted to say, but she didn't dare.

"What do you do? Like work, man. Are you a preacher or something?"

"I'm a coach at Hilltop College."

The fellow lowered the gun a couple of inches. "Honest, you work at the college?" Disbelief lined his voice.

"Yes, do you want to see our parking passes?"

"Yeah. Throw them up here."

Had he gotten the guy's interest—in a good way? Ruthie dug her college parking pass out of her purse with a trembling hand. Moose pulled his credentials out of his wallet, then tossed them both on the porch. When the man leaned down to pick them up, the rifle moved up and down.

While studying the passes, the man loosened his hold on the weapon, causing it to wobble. Ruthie pulled her elbows against her sides, trying to make herself less of a target of a misfire.

"They look real. You can come on the porch."

The man fidgeted, bobbling the firearm. "You sure you don't have a gun?"

"We're positive." With the fear the man might want to shoot them lessening, Ruthie intended to use her classroom voice to demand he put down the rifle. Her throat tightened at the sight of the unsteady barrel though.

She and Moose walked onto the porch together. When she got a good look at the person standing at the door, she rubbed her eyelids, then blinked. She punched Moose's arm and whispered, "He's so young. Why he could pass for one of my students."

Moose nodded. "Yes."

"Put down the bags," the kid demanded.

Moose and Ruthie did as he said. The young man opened them and rummaged through them with his right hand while trying to balance the restless rifle under his left arm.

Ruthie turned to Moose. "If he doesn't shoot us on purpose, he's going to do it by accident."

A faint snort shot out of Moose's nose. Did he sense something that made him think everything was alright now? "You won't laugh if that thing goes off."

"You're right."

Finally, the young man finished his search. "Turn

your pockets inside out."

Ruthie looked at Moose.

He nodded, and they emptied their pockets.

"Well, come in. I was making a pot of coffee when I heard something outside. You want a cup?"

After they picked up the loose change and keys and followed the kid, Moose seemed less anxious. He knew young men. What had Moose discerned about this guy? Had the kid's harsh attitude been out of fear of them? Maybe. Ruthie wouldn't let down her guard though. "Get rid of the gun." She refused to take one step while he held a firearm.

The young man fidgeted. The weapon wiggled. "Yeah, okay." He propped it beside the door.

Ruthie had a vision of steam wafting from a huge coffee cup. She could smell the aroma. "I'll pay for the coffee."

The guy's eyebrows arched. "No need. You can have it." He looked at Moose. "How about you?"

"Yes, I'd like a cup too if you can spare it."

Moose and Ruthie grabbed their belongings. The kid picked up his rifle and opened the oak paneled front door. Seeing the threshold as a dangerous barrier, Ruthie didn't budge. The young man held up the gun, and she backed away.

"Don't worry. I'm just bringing it inside. See." He walked indoors and set the gun in the foyer.

Only then did Ruthie enter and follow him and Moose to a rustic living area furnished with a brown leather sofa, matching easy chair, and a recliner. A flat screen television hung on the wall facing them. A large brick fireplace nearly filled a wall to the left. They continued to a kitchen with hardwood floors, granite countertops, and stainless-steel appliances.

"You can leave your bags on the floor."

Ruthie scrutinized the kid, who got three mugs out of the cabinet as she and Moose dropped their luggage. Ruthie looked around the room and pinched herself. She wasn't dreaming. She was in a real house.

"Have a seat." The kid motioned toward a couple of chairs at a picnic style table.

Moose and Ruthie sat down. Then the kid placed cream, sugar, and napkins in front of them. He joined them, then pulled Ruthie and Moose's parking passes from his blue jean pocket, and placed them on the table.

Gurgles from the coffee maker stopped. The guy got up and put a cup in front of Ruthie, the hazelnut smell tickling her nostrils. "I can hardly believe I'm looking at this delectable hot coffee."

The young man's throat resonated with low laughter, then questioning lines creased his brow as though he didn't know what to think or say.

She spooned in sugar, sipped, and let the smooth liquid line her throat. As her taste buds exploded with happiness, she grasped the cup with both hands and dared anyone to pry it from her. "Thank you so much."

"You're welcome. You can have all you want." Their host continued to gaze at her for a few minutes, then directed his attention to Moose as though he tried to size them up.

Moose, who picked up his coffee and took one swallow after another, seemed oblivious to the once over he got. Eventually, he put his cup down and looked directly at the kid. "Thank you for your kindness. Tell us a little about yourself."

Ruthie was glad Moose asked. Curiosity and

uncertainty burned a hole in her thoughts. What did a young person do in these woods for a livelihood, fun, or anything else? He didn't seem reclusive. Why wasn't he in college or out working?

The kid cocked an eyebrow. "Why not? I'm Thad Smith. Thad is short for Thaddeus."

Moose and Ruthie extended their hands and Thad shook them.

"It's nice to meet you. As you probably saw on my parking pass, my given name is George, but my friends and the kids I coach call me Moose."

"You really a coach?"

Moose sat straight up. "Yes."

Thad scooted forward. "What kind? I mean what sport?"

"Football."

"No way, you're not just fooling me?"

"No. My players and I use the gear in one of those bags you searched."

"I mostly felt around to check for a gun."

"Look again." Moose pointed toward his luggage.

Thad hopped up, brought the bag to the table, and pulled out a football. Looking like a kid on Christmas morning, he sat down with it, rolling it around in his hands, rubbing it. "Hey man, this is great."

Hearing enthusiasm in Thad's voice, Ruthie relaxed and scanned her surroundings. How could a young man afford this place? Why would he want to live in the wilderness in the winter? There had to be a reason, such as he didn't own this house, but stayed here to watch after it for someone. She sucked in a puff of air. What if he committed a crime and ran from the law?

Chapter Sixteen

Ruthie finished her coffee and set her cup on the kitchen table. As her eyelids grew heavy, her chin slid down, but she snapped it up. She had to stay awake. Her and Moose's lives could depend on it. Even though Thad sounded friendly, she couldn't get the image of his gun pointed at her and Moose out of her mind.

"So..." Moose directed his attention to Thad. "Do you play football?"

"Me?" Thad placed his forefinger on his chest. "Nah, not anymore."

"What types of things do you enjoy?" Ruthie asked.

"I like athletics. I played a little football in high school. When I entered college this past fall, my dad insisted I put all my effort into my grades."

Moose tapped his finger on his cup. "I think sports build character and self-confidence. I'd recommend them for any student."

"Dad doesn't see it that way. He insisted I make the honor roll at the University of North Carolina." Thad let out a chuckle lined with sarcasm. "If he had his way, I'd graduate as the valedictorian."

Ruthie related to trying to live up to someone else's high expectations, but her parents would never have cast her into a place so desolate and cold. What happened? "How did you end up here?"

"My father didn't approve of my first semester grades, so he sent me here to get my priorities straight."

Ruthie let out a tiny gasp. "My parents mapped out my academic upbringing, so I have some idea of what you're going through."

"How did your parents' plan turn out for you?"

"Okay. I'm a college professor and enjoy my students." She smoothed the front of her shirt. "However, each person's situation is unique. People are different. You should consider your talents and interest. I would like to go back in time, socialize more, and study less. I'm sometimes ill at ease in large groups."

Ruthie had buried those true words in her heart. They'd never popped out before, but maybe saying them would help Thad. Then again, she had to remember. Thad's dad wasn't her mom or dad. "Don't let me interfere in decisions made between you and your father. I'm sure he's thinking of your best interest. Yet, you're the one who will get up and go to whatever job you choose for at least twenty years, maybe longer."

Thad steepled his fingers. "It's a lot to think about."

If Ruthie's frank admission about her uneasiness in large groups shocked Moose, he didn't let on. Instead, he directed his attention to Thad. "We all have something in common. My father wanted me to follow in his footsteps as an Army Colonel."

Thad's eyebrows headed for his hairline. "You

didn't do it?"

"No." The strength of steel lined Moose's words. "And I'm glad I didn't. I love my job."

Thad hopped up as though he needed a break to decipher the conversation. "Want some more coffee?"

Moose and Ruthie held out their cups.

"Thank you," Ruthie said. She couldn't get enough of the pick-me-up.

As Thad poured, he gave Moose and Ruthie a questioning look? "Have you eaten?"

Ruthie nearly came out of her seat at the mention of food. She didn't want to impose, but she refused to ponder whether giving them something to eat would inconvenience him. "No, we haven't."

"You want a cheese sandwich?"

"That would be wonderful. I'll pay..." She glanced at Moose. "We'll both pay."

"No problem. I've had the cheese a while. I need to finish it before it molds." He walked to the kitchen counter. After pulling a frying pan from the cabinet, he twirled it around and sang a catchy tune. Moving his shoulders and hips, he danced in place as he stood at the stove preparing their dinner.

Ruthie couldn't imagine sticking a friendly, outgoing kid in these hills in the winter. Yet, there was the gun. How well adjusted was he? Hmm. They probably frightened him when they appeared out of this deserted forest. What was his father thinking?

The smell of butter and cheese wafted over the table and set her taste buds on fire. Eating overtook her thoughts. When Thad served the food, she looked at Moose.

He scooted up to the table and nodded.

She bowed her head.

"Our Heavenly Father, thank you for bringing us safely to Thad's and for his generosity. Bless this food to the nourishment of our bodies and protect us as we travel. In Christ's name we pray. Amen."

Restraining herself from tearing into her sandwich, Ruthie munched on the first bite. "Oh my, this is delicious." That was an understatement. It was the most scrumptious sandwich she'd ever eaten. "You're so kind."

"Yes, thank you." Pure joy resonated in Moose's tone.

"You're welcome." Thad sat in his chair and said nothing while Ruthie and Moose ate.

Ruthie tried not to gobble up the rest of her food, but the way Thad gazed at her as though she was the hungriest person he'd ever seen, she figured she had failed.

"So, what do you think about living here in winter?" Moose swallowed a bite of his sandwich.

Ruthie sat at attention as she chewed. Good question. Staying here all alone seemed more like a punishment than a retreat for meditation, not to mention the danger of running into an escaped criminal.

Thad sipped his coffee. "According to my father, after I spend the winter here, I'll realize my destiny in life, so I suppose it's worth it, but it's no fun."

Ruthie let out a little gasp. Maybe Thad's father didn't realize what this place was like this time of year. Surely, he didn't know about Hucklesford. "Did he tell you what your calling should be?"

"He wants me to pull up my grades, major in business, and become an officer in his company after I learn the inner workings of every department from the bottom up."

Moose held his sandwich in mid-air. "You're here all day with nothing to do, right?"

Thad shrugged. "I go to the grocery in the snow, watch television, and play video games."

"Since you're sitting out a semester, would your father object to your working at Hilltop College and setting your priorities there instead of here?"

Thad shot up like someone set off a firecracker underneath him. "Possibly not, but he doesn't want me to continue my education until I declare a worthwhile major and settle down enough to make all A's and B's. I would work hard to do that to keep the job at Hilltop."

Glancing between Thad and Moose, Ruthie tried to keep up with the conversation, which flew back and forth as fast as a volley in a tennis match. Still, the gist of it sank in. A job at Hilltop would get Thad out of this frozen forest, away from Hucklesford, and around kids his age. "Would the owner of the house object to your leaving early?"

Thad smiled. "My father owns it, but what could I do at Hilltop?"

Now Ruthie understood why Thad, at his young age, lived in a fine house in this remote area, but for the life of her, she still couldn't see the sense in it.

Moose put down his sandwich. "My student team manager graduated early, so I'm looking for a new one. Student assistants arrive at the college before each semester starts, so you could assist at our bowl game and help with after-the-season duties."

Thad hit the table so hard, he jarred it.

Ruthie and Moose grabbed their coffee cups.

"You serious, man?"

Moose blinked. "Yes, I am."

"I like that idea."

"If your dad would go along with it, you could enroll in Hilltop College's business management program, then transfer to UNC in a couple of years."

"Man, I'm so glad she saw this house and the two of you came here." He gave Moose a high-five. "I think you just got my priorities straight for me."

Moose and Ruthie chuckled for the first time since they'd set foot inside Thad's home. Then Ruthie ate the last bite of her sandwich and sipped her coffee while Moose and Thad went over the salary for the job.

Moose offered to contact admissions for Thad for Spring Semester and told Thad what he needed to submit. "As soon as you apply online, I'll speed up the process." Moose grunted. "Providing my phone will work."

"Neither my cell nor the landline in the master bedroom has worked since the storm." Thad rose in his chair and looked toward the window. "It's still snowing."

"That's good. It will cover our tracks." Ruthie folded the corner of her napkin.

"You don't think the criminal followed you to the house, do you?" Thad glanced at Ruthie, then Moose.

"I hate to admit it, but we only thought of getting help." He let his eyes meet Thad's. "It didn't occur to me that whoever lived here wouldn't have phone service. I assumed we'd knock on the door and the resident would call the authorities. In hindsight, I regret our tunnel vision. I don't want to put you in danger. We better get going."

"No, I can't turn you out. As I said, I'm a Christian. I can see my mom pointing her finger at me saying, 'Thaddeus, don't you dare send those poor people outside in this weather.'" Thad arched an eyebrow. "If the snow's covering your tracks, there's no reason to think he'd look here." He gulped. "Is there?"

"I'm not sure. We may have confused him about the direction we took at a steep, rocky slope." Moose shook his head. "He's stayed on our trail so far though."

Moose stood, and Ruthie joined him.

"We're getting out of here before we put you in danger. Thank you for your kindness." Moose offered Thad his hand.

Thad jumped up. "No, don't leave. What if he comes and you're not here? I'll have to fight him off alone."

Moose and Ruthie sat down.

"It looks as though we may have brought a hoodlum to your door, even though we didn't mean to," Ruthie said.

"Yeah but, he might have come around here looking for you even if you hadn't stopped by. I'm glad you're here. Do either of you know anything about him?" Thad's voice cracked.

Ruthie leaned forward. "Not much. His name is Damian Hucklesford. According to the news, he robbed a jewelry store and killed three people."

Thad wrung his hands.

"The radio announcer said the police described him as a thirty-year-old former gang member with a trim build, a beard, and long black hair. He was last seen wearing a motorcycle jacket and black pants, possibly taking refuge in these mountains." Ruthie fought to hold on to what strength she had left while talking about Hucklesford. "According to the man reporting, law enforcement searched the Appalachian Trail, but found no trace of him or clues leading to his whereabouts."

"I'd get the police up here if the phone worked. Since I can't, I'd rather take my chances with the two of you here. If he followed you, we'll probably find out tonight."

Chapter Seventeen

Moose drummed his fingers on the kitchen table, then he let his eyes meet Thad's. "If we stay here, we could put you in danger. If we go, we could put you in danger."

"Like I said, I don't want to be in this house alone with a killer out there. If the landline worked, I'd call my dad and tell him I'm leaving this desolate, forsaken place." Lifting his body an inch off of the chair, Thad looked out the window, then slouched. "It's snowing harder. You don't really want to hunt for a place to sleep in this weather when you could cut your zzz's in a nice, warm bed, do you?"

Moose could tell by Thad's desperate expression they could not leave him behind. Not only that, he was right. A bed for his aching body sounded like a dream come true.

"No, we don't," Ruthie said. "We appreciate your kind offer." She looked at Moose, then at Thad. "Since we are staying, would you let Moose have some ice? He fell and hurt his rib muscle and ankle."

"Why didn't you tell me? I'll get them now." Thad

got up and retrieved two gel packs from the freezer. "Here ya' go. I hope you feel better tomorrow."

Moose took them and held them up. "Thank you for these and for your offer of beds. We accept."

Thad flashed a wide smile. "I'm glad you're staying."

Moose considered several scenarios. In the worst one, Hucklesford followed them here, waited until they fell asleep, killed them, and took over the house. He bounced his leg. He couldn't let that happen.

His dad taught him to use a gun shooting tin cans. Afterward, he took him hunting, but Dad fired the bullets then. He'd inherited his mother's love of animals and never carried a weapon. He doubted Thad knew how to use his rifle the way it wobbled when he held him and Ruthie at gunpoint. He would have to handle Thad's rifle. "We need to make a plan for the night in case Hucklesford finds this place." He worked hard at keeping his voice calm.

Thad leaned across the table. "What do you suggest?"

"I'm a football coach, not a law enforcement officer, but I think we should take shifts sleeping. If something suspicious happens, the person on guard can wake the others, and...." Moose drew out the word and. "We need a plan to protect ourselves. Of course, we'll lock all of the windows and doors and stay away from the windows."

"Pull all the curtains or blinds shut." Ruthie pointed toward the back porch. "There's always the old way of putting heavy furniture in front of the doors."

Moose nodded. "We could do that. We'd hear him trying to move the items."

Thad touched his chin with his forefinger. "Could we set traps on the doorknobs?"

Moose couldn't imagine what they could use. Nails? How would they put nails on doorknobs?

Ruthie shot straight up. "Do you have anything glass we could break?"

"Yes. Mom asked me to clean out the cabinets and get rid of some old dishes."

"Perfect. Let's glue broken pieces of glass to sheets of plastic and make covers for the outside doorknobs," Ruthie said.

Moose clasped his hands together. "I like it. We'll hear him screaming if he grabs hold of that."

"You some kind of genius or something?" Thad leaned toward Ruthie.

She snickered. "I'm happy if I've helped, but it's probably something I read in a book."

"She's read plenty of them, but seriously, I like that suggestion. He won't notice anything amiss in the dark. Let's break the dishes on a large garbage bag to keep any stray pieces off of the floor."

Thad grinned. "I have everything we need. Give me a few minutes."

He left and returned with the supplies. Then he escorted Moose and Ruthie to the rustic back porch, where they broke the dishes. It took two hours, but by eleven forty-five they placed coverings bearing sharp pieces of glass on the doorknobs.

Thad brushed his hands together. "For defense, I have a cast iron frying pan, a hammer, and the rifle."

"That's a weapon for each of us. Three against one," Moose said.

"I hear ya.' Dad keeps the rifle here in case a rabid

animal gets inside or near the house. We don't even hunt, though. I know I held a gun on you two, but I know almost nothing about using it." He looked at Moose.

Moose let out a loud sigh. "I'll keep the rifle. If he shows up, I'll let him know we're armed."

Thad hopped up and gave Moose the rifle, along with spare bullets. Then he turned toward Ruthie. "If either of us hears anything, we'll wake him first."

"Okay." Ruthie gazed at Moose. "You'll get us up if anything happens on your watch, right?"

"Of course. Best scenario, he won't appear. If he attempts a break-in, it will take all of us to defend ourselves." Moose rubbed the butt of the rifle. He hoped firing into the air would scare Hucklesford away.

Ruthie looked at Thad. "I'll take the frying pan."

"All right." Thad pulled an iron skillet out of the cabinet and passed it to Ruthie. "I'll show you to your rooms, then get the hammer off of the back porch." He curved his arm, giving Moose and Ruthie a "follow me" motion.

He led them down a hall to two rooms across from each other. "They both have bathrooms. You're welcome to share or have a bedroom of your own."

"We'll each take one," Moose said. "Who wants what shift?"

Thad glimpsed his watch. "It's midnight. If we cover the next nine hours, that's three each. I'm used to staying up late watching old movies or playing video games to keep me company during the dark, lonely nights. I'll take the first turn from midnight until three in the morning and leave the volume on my new video game low."

Moose gave him a thumbs up. "I'll take the three o'clock shift." He glanced at Ruthie. "I'll get you up at six o'clock. I don't think Hucklesford would approach the house then, but the sun doesn't rise until seven-thirty this time of year, so stay alert." Moose glanced at Thad, then Ruthie. "If nothing happens, let me and Thad sleep until we wake up, right Thad?"

Thad smiled big. "Right."

"Since I drew the prize and get six straight hours of sleep, if it's all right with Thad, I'll look for something in the kitchen to fix for lunch."

"Great," Thad said.

"I'll take the bedroom I'm standing beside and see you later." Moose walked into the room, shut the door, and collapsed on the bed.

~

Exhausted, Ruthie couldn't get to her bedroom and private bath fast enough. She would never have dreamed a ten-by-twelve room with a standard-sized bed and a floral-designed comforter would look like paradise, but it did. She got in the shower and relished the warm water running over her. The moist heat seeped into every pore in her body. Even though she didn't want to get out, she finally cut off the showerhead and wrapped a towel around her. When she stepped on the plush bedroom carpet, she wiggled her toes. For the first time since she left Hilltop College, she pulled her pajamas out of her bag.

Touching them, she remembered their soft comfort and held the top against her cheek. It was a good thing Thad and Moose took the first two shifts because her eyelids were as heavy as the skillet Thad had given her. She got into bed, pulled up the covers, and went to sleep as soon as she lay down.

She woke when someone roused her.

"Ruthie, get up. It's five-forty-five. Your shift starts in fifteen minutes."

"Huh?" Where was she?

"He hasn't shown up so far," Moose whispered.

Ruthie groaned as she remembered coming to Thad's. "We must've thrown him off at the scree slope."

"I hope so. The hall and kitchen nightlights are on. As soon as you're settled, turn off the one in the kitchen."

"Right."

After Moose left, Ruthie put on a clean pair of jeans and a T-shirt, and went to the kitchen. Remembering her commitment to prepare lunch, she poked around in the fridge and freezer. Thad had plenty of food, but she figured everyone liked hamburgers. When she and Moose ate the fish in the cave, she had promised herself she would put a burger in Moose's future. After she took out a pound of ground beef to thaw, satisfaction filled her. "There."

She poured a cup of coffee Moose or Thad had brewed, and her tastebuds danced. After turning off the nightlight, she sat down at the table. A faint beam from a tiny fixture shining nearby in the hall shed light into part of the room. The heat kicked on as she took the first sip of her drink. She propped her feet on the rung of a chair across from her, brought the cup to her lips, and swallowed—pure pleasure.

She knew the chilliness of the outdoors only too well. Since she and Moose had gone to sleep with a fire burning, she hadn't faced complete darkness. Outside the black night poured into the room through the kitchen window. With the cloud cover over the moon and stars, not one flicker of light shone to illuminate Hucklesford if he hid in the inky shield. Ruthie yearned for even one star to twinkle, to take her from the depths of aloneness and the evil she sensed. She made no noise and tuned her ears to the outdoor sounds, absolute quiet surrounding her until she heard a crunch.

Chapter Eighteen

Ruthie inched around in her seat at the kitchen table. As heavy footsteps broke through the ice, her pulse pounded in her temples. She put her hands over her ears. The ice cracked. The steps plodded through the quiet as though someone dragged them. Ruthie sat straight up, inclining her ear toward the window. A large object hit the ice.

She jumped. An animal looking for food? Yes. One of those catamounts. Shivering, she rocked—waiting. At first light, she'd see the creature's footprints. The dark night wrapped around her. Glued to her seat, she focused on the blackness as though a light would shine through and bring her hope if she looked at it long enough.

At last, it did. The sun painted pink streaks across the sky. Bright rays played around an object on the window. Ruthie leaned forward and gasped—the red button from her coat. Weak, she slid until she clutched the bottom of her seat and righted her position.

She had to remove the button to show Hucklesford they stood on alert. What if he saw the glass traps on the doorknobs? She had to take those off too. She stood on wobbly legs and stepped toward the door. A hand grasped her from behind. She screamed.

Moose whispered. "It's me. Anything happening?"

Ruthie swallowed the knot the size of her coffee cup in her throat and pointed to the window. "He's out there." She couldn't keep her voice from quivering. "I almost woke you after I heard crunching, but I told myself it was an animal. Deep down, I didn't believe it. I knew it was Hucklesford, but that's what I told myself." She sucked in air and strangled. After a coughing spell, she said, "We have to get the traps off of the doorknobs. He'll see them in broad daylight. If we need to use them again, he won't grasp one."

"When did you hear the noise?"

"Right after I got here, about six."

"Don't worry. I doubt he noticed our little surprises in the dark. I'll remove them in case he returns."

"He also left the button from my coat taped on a window."

Moose's eyes widened. "Wow! He did get close to the house. Why didn't he break in?"

"I don't know."

"Wait here." Moose went outside.

Ruthie held her stomach as her nerves unraveled like a worn towel coming apart one thread at a time. Would she hear Hucklesford's rifle? Would he shoot…? Was Moose alright? *Please, Lord, take care of Moose.*

Finally, Moose walked in carrying the plastic traps and the button.

Ruthie hopped up. He placed the items on the kitchen table, embraced her, and lightened her worry.

"I'm glad to see you."

As soon as the words left Ruthie's mouth, Moose closed his eyelids part of the way and hugged her as though he didn't want to let go.

Even though his presence brought comfort, the thankfulness didn't settle her scattered thoughts. What should she and Moose do next? What could Moose do? After all, he had taken a terrible fall. "What do you think about Hucklesford? And how are you? Did the icepacks help?"

Moose flicked her nose with his forefinger. "After using the icepacks several times during the night, I'm much better. The ankle and the rib muscles are a little sore, but nothing compared to what they were. As for Hucklesford, he's probably watching the house. However..." Moose held up his forefinger like a professor making a point. "I think I know why he didn't break in. He doesn't know who lives here—a hunter, backwoodsman, forest ranger, or even a policeman. I lay you ten to one—he won't try anything until he finds out who's in here."

"That's true, but after all he's done, does he really care?"

"Sure. The last thing he wants to do—break in and confront an armed law enforcement officer. Let's have some coffee. Then I'll help with that meal you promised. Looking at the food thawing on the counter, I can't believe a chunk of raw ground beef's making my mouth water. We'll eat as soon as it's ready, even if it's burgers for brunch. Then hopefully, we can escape before Hucklesford realizes it's just us and a kid."

Ruthie poured two cups of coffee with her hand shaking. Dodging and out-maneuvering Hucklesford was like a game, a very dangerous game. After they sat down at the table, she asked, "Where will we go?"

"Out of here if Thad can tell us the way. When I placed the plastic trap on the back porch doorknob, I noticed a 2000 ¾--ton pickup. I'll drive it to civilization."

Ruthie held onto her seat, this time to keep from floating off of it. "How wonderful. Do you think Thad will agree? It's ten o'clock, but we promised not to wake him."

"We won't. However, I imagine the aroma of brunch cooking will. Let's get started."

"Okay." Ruthie stood. "I found a bag of peas and pre-cut French fries in the freezer. Do you want those?"

"I could eat the bags."

Ruthie giggled and tried to soak in the confidence and calm Moose exhibited. If she let fear overtake her, she couldn't think straight and she needed her wits about her. "All right, as soon as I mix the main dish, I'll start the veggies."

By eleven o'clock, the aroma of hamburgers and French fries wafted through the kitchen, and sure enough, Thad appeared.

He grinned big. "Hey, mornin.' It smells like the neighborhood diner back home."

Moose turned to face him. "Where is home?"

"We're in a suburb of Charlotte, the Queen City."

"A great place. What does your father's company do?"

Thad sidled to the stove and checked out the food. "Design computer systems."

Moose whistled. "That's lucrative."

"My dad's done well. He wants me to enjoy the

same lifestyle he and Mom have. I've interned at the company in summers since high school." Wrinkles creased Thad's brow. "I don't like it."

"Most people have to spend a major portion of their lives at work. They should do something they enjoy." Moose grimaced. "I spoke out of turn. It's none of my business."

"That's pretty much what I think, but my opinion gets buried in my father's wishes. After working hard to build a successful company, he's convinced he's ensured a good future for me if I continue what he started. I get that. He's a great guy—smart too. It's just not the career for me."

Ruthie set a plate of burgers on the table. "Let's eat."

Moose directed his attention to her. "You won't have to tell me twice. Can I help?"

As Ruthie spun toward the stove, she looked over her shoulder. "Sure. Set the table and get our drinks. I made sweet tea."

In only moments, they sat down, and Moose said a blessing.

As soon as they raised their heads, he directed his gaze to Thad. "I noticed a truck outside."

"Yeah, it's mine." Thad turned his attention to the food as though he didn't welcome the interruption.

Moose took a bite of his burger and laid it down. "I could drive it down the mountain if it's all right with you, and you could tell me the way out of here."

Thad held his burger in mid-air. "In this weather?" Disbelief resounded in his words.

Ruthie picked up a French fry. "Yes, I don't want to spoil the rest of your lunch, and I'm sorry to tell you, but the guy following us has shown up."

Thad sprang out of his chair. "How do you know?"

She explained about the button from her coat.

Thad hit the table with the palm of his hand. "I don-don-don't believe this."

"Let's eat, then we'll leave." Moose spoke with a strong steady voice. "Don't worry, son. We brought this to your doorstep. We'll get you to safety."

Thad sat down. "It's not your fault. Like I said, he might have come anyway." The tendons in his neck stuck out as he gulped down his burger. "Let's go. I'll get the rifle."

Ruthie cringed.

"We need to think this through and make a plan. When did you last drive the truck?" Moose asked.

Thad flicked his fork up and down on his plate. "Ah, let me think. Not long, just a couple of days ago. After the storm hit, but before the road turned to solid ice, I went to the truck stop to buy a new video game."

Ruthie finished her meal and picked up the dishes.

Moose stood and turned toward her. "I'll wash those."

Thad hopped up and snatched the ketchup. "Yeah, let's clean this up and get out of here."

In no time, it seemed the kitchen sparkled. Not used to a full meal, Ruthie grew sleepy. She forced her eyelids open though and directed her gaze to Thad. "If only we could call the police. I assume you checked the landline."

Thad's lips turned down. "Yeah. There's no dial tone."

Ruthie pointed toward the window. "It's snowing so hard I can barely see outdoors."

"That's exactly the cover I need to check out the truck." Moose darted to Thad. "Can I use your keys?"

"Sure." Thad pulled his key fob from his pocket and handed it to Moose.

Moose rushed outside, the door slamming behind him.

Ruthie watched him remove the protective cover from the cab of the truck and get in the driver's seat, but she didn't hear the engine. She pressed her nose against the kitchen window. The snow picked up making it difficult to see outside. She bit her fingernail. If Moose didn't come indoors soon, she would go out to look for him.

Finally, he appeared like a vision stepping out of a white curtain. After he entered the house, he snatched off his knit hat and ran his hand through his hair. "The handle's iced over. I need hot water."

Ruthie quickly filled a pan for him and stood at the window with Thad watching until Moose disappeared in the thick snow. Surely, she would hear the engine turning over soon. But no. She charged outdoors and ran into Moose heading toward the house. Stamping his feet at the kitchen door, he knocked white flakes off of his boots.

Thad rubbed his palms against each other. "What do you think, man?"

Moose pressed his lips so tight they formed a straight line. "I can't start it."

"So, what's wrong? Fix it." Thad's voice rose.

"I'm not sure if I can. It's a 2015 truck, right?"

"Yes, it's kinda' old, but it always works. I can't believe…" Thad's eyebrows formed a V over his nose. "I can't believe it's not running today of all days."

"It's probably cold or has a bit of ice in the battery. Believe it or not, they can freeze, but this one has no cracks or bulges, so I doubt it's frozen."

Thad paced around the room. "We have to get out of here."

Ruthie gave Thad a hug. "Moose will get us out."

"I'll help. Just tell me what to do, man." Thad cut his eyes at Moose.

"Pack a bag with plenty of warm clothes while I decide the best way to deal with this."

"All right, but just so you know, I have a charger we can use on the battery."

"Great news, but we have to warm the battery first." Moose snapped his fingers. "Uh, Thad, do you have a multimeter we could use to check the voltage. We might not need to charge it."

"Yeah, I do."

"Okay. We'll leave the battery in the truck and use Ruthie's hairdryer if you have a long extension cord."

"Uh-Uh. Yes." Thad darted out of the room. Returning within minutes, he held up the cord and handed Moose the multimeter.

Ruthie rushed to her bag in the bedroom, pulled out her hair dryer, and charged to the back porch. As Thad plugged in the extension cord, Ruthie tapped her foot. After she attached the hairdryer to the cord, she stretched it as far as it would go. "Yes." She jumped up and down.

Moose zipped out the door, Ruthie following. He raised the hood and started the process while Ruthie held an umbrella and ran a scraper over the driver's side of the windshield as fast as she could. Scraping, Moose blowing, her scraping. It seemed to go on forever.

"How much longer?"

"Probably ten to twenty minutes."

"Sounds good." Ruthie directed her gaze to the right, then the left. "The snow's dissipating."

A bullet dinged the truck's hood.

Weakness surged through Ruthie like a river. She dropped the umbrella. The scraper nearly fell, but she tightened her grip. She wanted to finish the job. Their escape depended on getting the battery to work and scraping the windshield.

Chapter Nineteen

Ruthie stood beside the truck and stared at the snow-covered forest to her left, searching for an enemy she couldn't see.

"Get inside the house." Moose punctuated each syllable with a tone as strong as steel.

"Not until you do." Ruthie blinked away tears soaking her eyelashes.

"We have to leave here. I have to warm up..."

Another bullet hit the hood. Moose closed it.

He clasped Ruthie's hand and they ran, slipping and sliding. As they reached the backdoor, three bullets struck to their right.

Thad, who stood in the kitchen holding the rifle, poked the bobbling weapon toward Moose. "Here."

Pointing the rifle up, Moose fired out the door at nothing. "He knows we're armed. He's probably seen the three of us and guessed there are no rangers or policemen here." Moose put the rifle in the corner. "More than likely, he'll try to catch us at a window, or he'll wait and break in tonight."

Deep muscle shakes rattled Ruthie.

Thad pulled a chair up to the table and sat down.

Moose and Ruthie joined him.

"How can he see us with the blinds and curtains drawn?" Thad bounced his knee.

"When the sun starts to set, we'll make shadows. We have a while though. It's only four-thirty." Moose sounded matter-of-fact.

Ruthie shook her foot while she waited to hear Moose's plan. He appeared stalwart, but did his insides race? Finally, she asked, "What time should we leave?" She couldn't keep her voice from cracking.

"If we go to the truck, he'll shoot us," Thad said.

"If he sees us." Moose glanced at Ruthie then Thad. "I'm praying for a thick cover of snow. When it comes, I'll fix the battery. Count on it. Look in the cabinets for canned or non-perishable food. Pack what you can in case the battery dies, and we end up on foot."

Thad crossed his arms on the kitchen table and lay his head on them.

Ruthie resisted the urge to join him. Instead, she tapped his shoulder. "We have to keep fighting for our lives, praying, and believing we'll make it."

Thad raised up. He couldn't have had more pain on his face if she and Moose had beaten him. Yet he stood when she did. After they gathered the items Moose requested, Thad walked to the counter. "I'll make coffee." As he spooned the grounds, his hands shook so badly he spilled them all over the counter.

Ruthie cleaned them up and finished the task.

Glancing back and forth between the door and the window, Ruthie drank her pick-me-up standing at the counter. By five o'clock she finished it. Then, she concocted pimento cheese sandwiches, making extra for the trip. "Let's go ahead and eat. We'll call it an early dinner."

Moose and Thad joined her, all of them standing in silence, peering outside as they munched. Ruthie ate her last bite, gazing out, wishing, hoping, praying for thick, white snowflakes.

When Moose and Thad cleaned their plates, Ruthie put away the dishes and wiped the counter clean before she handed them the to-go sandwiches. "We'll take these with us. Let's fill our thermoses with coffee." She turned toward Thad. "Do you have one?"

"Yes." He took one from the cabinet. "There's a twenty-four pack of water bottles on the porch. I'll get it."

"Good idea," Moose said as he glanced at his watch, then the blinds. "The sun's setting. I'm going to work on the truck soon, heavy snow or not."

Right before darkness fell, snowflakes drifted from the sky.

Ruthie raised her hands heavenward. "Thank you."

Moose hopped up and dashed to the back porch, where he grabbed Ruthie's hair dryer still plugged into the extension cord. Right on his heels, she snatched the windshield scraper, followed him to the truck, and picked up the umbrella.

Moose opened the hood, then repositioned his toboggan. "Hopefully, the battery's not colder, or partially frozen, because Hucklesford forced us to stop blowing heat on it. If it's still somewhat warm, we'll only need ten or fifteen minutes." He turned on the hair blower, moving it across the battery, while Ruthie scraped ice off of the windshield.

With her heart beating against her ribs, she

hunched over, trying to morph into a smaller target. Hucklesford probably lurked somewhere watching their every move, listening to their words. She scrubbed so fast her hand blurred. As soon as she saw the seats inside the truck through the glass, she leaned toward Moose. "Check it now."

Moose got out the multimeter. "We're good." He slid in the truck and started it. "Let's get out of here." He hopped out and shut the hood.

Happiness bubbled in Ruthie's stomach like a fizzing soft drink as she followed Moose inside the house.

Thad stood inside, wringing his hands.

Crack. Crack. Thud.

Moose gritted his teeth. "Let's go. We're leaving."

"Do-do, you think it's safe?" Ruthie could barely speak over the fear mounting inside her.

"Yeah, man, maybe we should wait until he leaves."

"He won't leave. I'll take one last look under the hood to make sure everything's okay, then start the truck. Grab the bags and run for it as soon as you hear the engine. We'll have cover from the thick snow and twilight." Moose looked heavenward. "And, God's protection."

Judging from the fire dancing in Moose's eyes, trying to convince him to wait would've done no good.

He dashed out of the house toward the truck.

While Ruthie watched him prop a flashlight on the hood, she prayed. "Thank you, Lord, for sending snow. I can still see Moose's outline. Please create more precipitation to shield him. I ask in Jesus' name. Amen."

"Amen." Thad danced around like a nervous mosquito.

In minutes, a floodgate of big, white flakes fell from the sky, covering Moose like a blanket. Even though Ruthie had a bead on Moose's position, she couldn't make out his silhouette. The engine roaring came through loud and clear though, music to her ears.

The sound of freedom.

Thad picked up his and Moose's bags while Ruthie held hers in front of her to help her balance as she raced to the truck with her nerves as revved up as the engine. She and Thad tossed the luggage underneath the tarp over the truck's bed and piled in the front seat. She took a deep breath. "We're leaving. We're actually leaving." Joy exploded inside her.

"Yes, we're off." Moose practically sang the words.

Thad scooted in beside Ruthie. "I'm glad you're nice and trim, or we would've had to leave you here." He uttered a soft chuckle.

Ruthie laughed.

As soon as Thad shut the door, Moose leaned across Ruthie and asked, "All right, navigator, which way?"

"Go to the right. You can't see the driveway because it's getting darker outside and there's so much snow. We'll eventually merge with the two-lane road leading to the main highway."

Moose rubbed his hands around the steering wheel, then pulled away from the house. "We're out of here."

Bursting with happiness, Ruthie paid little attention to the truck weaving.

Thad scooted up in his seat then turned his head

toward Moose. "Past the next curve, there's a cliff on your side of the road. Slow down now. It's best to creep along that area. For several years, Dad has talked about putting up a guardrail, but no one's ever here in bad weather—until now."

As Moose stepped on the brakes, the truck skated to the right within an inch of a tree.

Ruthie placed her hands on the dashboard to brace herself. She glanced at Thad.

He swiped his hand across his brow. "That was close, man. You gotta' bring it down more."

"I'm only going fifteen miles an hour. If I slow down much, we'll stop." Moose rounded a curve too fast.

The truck spun.

Ruthie's arms flew up.

Thad recoiled in his seat.

Going with the slide, Moose held his foot on the brake and turned the wheel until they stopped.

Thad sat as still as a statue. "I'll assess our position."

"Good idea." Moose only said two words.

Ruthie heard stress in each of them.

Moose sucked in air, then exhaled. "I put a flashlight on the floorboard. It probably rolled under your seat."

Thad bent over and grabbed it. "Yep," he said as he got out.

He glided over ice in front of the truck's lights, flapping his arms until he steadied himself. Then he bent over long enough to examine the front wheels. As he trudged toward the rear of the vehicle, he braced himself against the truck bed.

After several minutes, he returned. "Part of the left rear wheel is…It's… over the edge. You probably need to gun the engine to get back on solid ground." Thad gulped. "When you do, there's no telling where we'll end up."

Ruthie stared out the windshield as the wipers thumped away snowflakes.

Moose grasped the steering wheel, then tightened his grip. "Brace yourselves. I'm going for it."

Ruthie held her breath. *Oh, Lord, please.*

Moose mashed the gas pedal. The wheel bumped onto the driveway, the truck headed for the precipice.

Ruthie grabbed the steering wheel and pulled to the right with Moose as hard as she could.

The truck fishtailed.

The white world flashed back and forth like lightning.

Thad dropped the flashlight and put his hands over his head.

Ruthie let go of the steering wheel and put her face between her knees.

Grunting, Moose straightened the vehicle.

Ruthie rose up to check on him. He was paler than pale.

Thad threw up his hands. "Whew! We're past the cliff. The worst we can do from here to the highway—hit a tree."

Moose's facial muscles tightened as the car skated down the driveway, skidding to the left, then the right. While they bounced in their seats, splatters of light shot from the flashlight rolling around the floorboard. Ruthie picked it up and turned it off as she swallowed the bile in her throat to keep from throwing up.

Moose got control of the truck, then glanced at Thad. "How much longer on this thing?" Tiredness lined his tone.

"The entire driveway's two miles. I think the narrow curve, where we nearly slid over the cliff, is halfway."

"Really? We've traveled such a short distance.' Moose tapped his thumb on the steering wheel. "Hucklesford could still be out there."

Thad sprang up in his seat. "He couldn't keep up with us on foot, could he?"

Ruthie looked at Moose.

"Hmm. Well, maybe not."

Ruthie understood Moose's reluctance to add to Thad's anxiety. They couldn't guarantee Hucklesford wouldn't show up though. She twisted the strap on her purse. "We stopped at the edge of the cliff and slowed down to five or six miles per hour several times."

Thad let out a loud sigh. "So, what are you suggesting? We can't drive any faster on this road."

"Every time it appears we'll pull away from Hucklesford and these mountains, the hills yank us back like giant wads of gum sticking to us. I have no suggestions. I'm thinking out loud."

Moose shifted in his seat. "I'm keeping watch. If I spot him, I'll do all I can. Depending on the situation, I'm not sure how much that will be."

As they approached a lighted area, Thad plastered his face against the passenger's window. "We're almost there, but I saw something. Let's park in the clearing and decide our next move."

A rifle blasted, blowing out the right front tire.

Chapter Twenty

As the truck's tire lost air, it thumped on the icy road.

Ruthie swallowed the scream inside her.

"How much farther to a place to park?" Moose asked.

"We're almost there. It's…it's a sharp turn. Sloooow, slow down and swing a-a little to the left." Thad made a curving motion with his trembling hand.

Pieces of ice flew off of the road and danced in beams in front of the headlights as they reached the base of the mountain.

Thad leaned forward. "There's the road." He popped his knuckles. "I hope that stalking dirtbag's gone."

Moose maneuvered the truck into a parking lot, which spanned a hundred feet into the forest. Finally, he stopped near a picnic table, barbecue pit, and large trash can. Letting go of the steering wheel, he slumped.

Thad made the sign of a cross. "Thank. Thank. Thank you, Jesus."

Ruthie forced words through her tight throat. "Is this part of a public park?"

"Uh-huh. There's a building farther in the woods." Thad pointed to the right of the picnic area. "If we don't want to change the tire tonight, we can sleep there."

Moose shot up and banged his head on the top of the truck. "You have a spare tire?"

Moose's excitement ignited a flame of hope inside of Ruthie.

"Yeah, man. Is that all we need?"

"It's enough to get on the road."

"Dad sent me to the wilderness to get my priorities straight, but he made sure I had plenty of supplies."

Ruthie hoped Thad's dad realized what a good kid he had. "It sounds as though your father intended to take care of you." Ruthie drummed her fingers on her knee. "Of course, he hadn't counted on us."

"I'm glad you're here. If you want to know the truth, I'm glad I'm out of there. But, but… what about Hucklesford? Do you think he's still chasing us? Why isn't he firing at us now?"

Ruthie hugged him. "You're a blessing to us." She winced. "I assume Hucklesford's out there. Someone just shot out one of our tires."

Moose leaned around Ruthie. "Even though we don't hear him right now, you can bet he's there. I don't know why he isn't shooting at us, but I'll take the lull. Since the temperature dropped, my best guess—he's made camp for the night." Moose arched his eyebrows. "By the way, I agree with Ruthie. We're fortunate we met you. Let's change the tire and go from there."

As soon as they got out of the truck, Moose squatted down and held the flashlight for Thad while he put on the spare tire. After they finished and rose, Moose cracked up the ice with his boot.

Ruthie stretched. She had sat with her muscles wound as tight as a coil the entire trip. Even though it hadn't taken long, it had seemed like forever.

Moose glanced from Ruthie to Thad. "If we travel now, we'll get ahead of him, but we'll make a slow, dangerous trip in the dark on a slippery road. What do the two of you think about resting?"

"It's up to you, man. We probably should leave, but we don't want to have a wreck doing it." Thad tsked his tongue. "You gotta' be tired."

"How far is the building?" Ruthie asked.

Thad put his hands on Ruthie's shoulders, then pointed a flashlight into the night. "If you look through the fog and snow, there's a faint outline of a square as though someone painted it there. See it?"

Ruthie narrowed her eyes. "I think so."

Moose checked his watch. "It's too early to bed down. Let's see what the place offers."

Ruthie detected exhaustion in Moose's voice. "Good idea."

"I'll bring the bags in case we decide to stay." Thad started toward the truck.

Moose followed him using a labored gait, probably from pain in the muscles he strained when he fell down the scree. Not to mention how tiring the stress of keeping them from sailing over a cliff must've been.

After Thad and Moose snatched the bags, Moose handed Thad a flashlight. "Lead the way."

Accustomed to holding onto tree limbs to maintain her balance, Ruthie grasped the low-hanging branches on the skeleton hardwood trees and pines laden with icicles as she planted one foot in front of the other. The animals that rustled the underbrush and broke twigs during the day had taken refuge, the silence making it seem she, Moose, and Thad were the only living creatures outside. One other person was out here, though.

Ruthie trudged across the frozen snow at a slow pace as did Moose and Thad. Going onward on little energy, it seemed as though she had walked through the wilderness for hundreds of miles before the spotty outline of the structure appeared amid the fog and snowflakes.

She checked her watch—eleven o'clock, her bedtime before she wrecked her car and fled from a murderer in this forest. She clapped. "We can sleep indoors. Yay." There was no reason they couldn't stay here, was there? "Have you seen this place inside?" She turned toward Thad.

"No, but I don't think anyone lives here."

"It doesn't appear occupied. If it's on public property, the area's citizens probably use it. Where I'm from, the county rents several buildings to locals for cookouts and parties." Suddenly, Moose's voice trailed off. "Unfortunately, they keep them locked."

Thad slapped his forehead. "I didn't think about that."

Moose shifted his weight and switched the bags to his other hand. His injured rib muscle probably ached after carrying them. He seemed to take it all in stride though. "It's okay. We'll figure it out."

All three of them shined flashlights on the structure, which had a rustic front porch and two large floor-to-ceiling windows.

Thad tried the door. "It's locked, of course." He sagged against it. "What have I done?"

"Nothing. We're okay. Maybe the windows are open." Moose tilted his chin upward as though he tried to use it to raise the windows by remote control.

Thad pushed up on the one on the right, grunted, then tried the one on the left. He turned around. "Nope."

"Check the windows in the back." Moose shifted his weight.

Thad walked out of sight, but his steps broke the ice. Then someone or something interrupted Thad's footfalls.

"Moose."

"Yes."

"Did you hear Thad going around the house? How about the extra steps? And then silence. The silence is worst of all."

"Everything's fine. More than likely, Thad roused an animal causing it to scamper away. As far as the silence, he must've gone too far away for us to hear him."

Maybe. Did Moose really believe Thad frightened an animal? She took him at his word and hoped he was right.

Erratic streaks of light pierced the dark. Ice crushing broke the quiet and Thad appeared, slipping and sliding. "There's one open window over the kitchen sink, but it's small."

Moose cocked an eyebrow and cut his gaze toward Ruthie. "Can she get through it?"

Ruthie bristled. "What?! You want me to do it? What if I get stuck? I'm not made of foam rubber, you know."

Moose flashed a big grin. "Definitely not." He held

up his forefinger as though he stressed a point to his football players. "But you are trim."

Moose was out, but Thad resembled a cross-country runner.

He pointed the flashlight to the right and lit the way, motioning for Moose and Ruthie to follow him. In several minutes, they stood beside a wooden shed.

Ruthie tried not to look at the two of them as though they were nuts, but her current assessment of them probably showed in her expression. "How do you expect me to get to it?"

"I climbed onto this storage unit." Thad lit up a narrow structure the same height as the house. "The distance between the two roofs can't be over six inches."

Since Thad knew the window was unlocked, he obviously had opened it. Did he even attempt to go indoors?

He placed his hand on the side of the shed. "From the top of here, I easily made my way to the window."

"Why didn't you go in?" Ruthie snapped at him.

Thad sputtered. "I tr-tr-truly tried, but I got stuck…sort of. Entering head first, I made it through the window's opening, then took hold of the kitchen counter. Unfortunately, I'm so tall I couldn't pull my legs inside to turn around. I had to retreat." He flapped his hands at Ruthie. "You're little and short. You can grasp the jamb at the top and go through."

"I'm afraid of heights."

A muscle twitched in Moose's cheek.

Thad adjusted the sleeves on his jacket. "You can do it." The authority of a forty-year-old judge lined Thad's tone.

Ruthie gritted her teeth at his audacity. He either didn't hear her, or ignored her.

"At least try. I'll get you down if you can't do it."

Moose had asked if she could fit through the window. She didn't want to let Moose down. Still, she didn't want to climb on the roof and break into a house. An arctic wind whipped around the corner of the building. The chill of night outdoors in this weather, the truth of their situation hit her like a two x four. She recalled all Moose had done to save their lives.

She focused on the shed and the house. As Thad had said—not too far apart. She could deal with the acrophobia, couldn't she? She let out a loud sigh. She couldn't live with herself if she didn't help. "All right." She gave Thad her sternest stare. "You must promise not to desert me."

"Are you kidding? Of course, I won't desert you."

Moose, who'd kept as quiet as the winter snow, wrinkled his brow. "Maybe you shouldn't do this, after all."

"I'm going to give it my best." Ruthie attempted to sound determined, but she heard her voice quiver.

Thad placed his palm on a rung of the ladder propped on the side of the storage unit. "Use this to get on the roof. After you're up there, I'll climb up part of the way, or all the way, to do whatever you need."

Ruthie took slow strides, then stepped on the first rung, hoping Thad's word was good. When she reached the top, she recalled a scene from her childhood, a day at the fair.

She had loved the first ride, the roller coaster. Still reeling from the rush of it, she joined her mom, who waited at the gate for her. On the next ride, the Ferris

Wheel, Mom climbed into the gondola with her.

Mom smiled when the wind blew on her face on the way to the top. Then she unleashed an airy laugh as they plunged downward. Ruthie loved the fun.

"I'm enjoying this," Mom had said before the ride swooped upward, jerked, and stopped with them at the highest point. They rocked with the breeze and Mom stiffened. Yet, she put her arm around Ruthie. "We're fine. They'll bring us down in a minute." But they couldn't start the machine. The blood drained from Mom's cheeks and she slumped.

Ruthie screamed so loud a man below hollered for her to hold on tight to her mom with one hand and the rail with the other, so neither of them would fall. No one could help until they finally started the ride. Ruthie had sobbed. Mom had gone to the hospital, where they had kept her overnight.

Thad took hold of Ruthie's waist and brought her back to the task. After he hoisted her, she crawled on all fours and whimpered uncontrollably.

Chapter Twenty-One

Ruthie's scalp tingled as she crawled on the roof of the shed.

"Don't look down. I'll move the ladder and stay right below you."

Thad's words sounded like babble to Ruthie, but he needed her. Moose needed her. She had to rise above her fear of heights to secure a warm, dry place for them for the night. If only she could summon enough courage to keep her heart from beating like a drum.

Finally, she reached the edge of the shed. She only had to step over six inches of thin air. That was nothing, right? She was too large to fall through the space. At worst, her leg might slip into it. It couldn't hurt as much as it did when she cut her leg on the beavers' dam, could it?

She stood and trembled, her leg wobbling as she raised her foot. Then, she slipped on the snowy rooftop. "No. No. Help. Help." She slid down.

"I got you. I got you." Thad shot from the top of the ladder and grabbed her waist. Then he hoisted her back onto the roof.

When Thad let go, she lay down in the snow. Only

a miracle could take her to the window.

"You're okay. Crawl to the edge, but don't stand until you're ready to walk over the space between the shed and the house. You'll only need to take one stride in the snow. It's fresh, so you should be able to walk in it. Let's try again."

Let's? What was he talking about? There was no let's.

Ruthie shuddered at what he and Moose had asked her to do. Good thing Thad had long arms to steady her, but thanks to his long legs, the job of getting in the window belonged to her. He wanted to do this? Sure he did. Deep inside, she yearned to help, to contribute, but not this way. Maybe something else later.

"Ready?"

No, she wasn't ready. She looked behind her. She'd made it over halfway across before she slipped. Now it was farther backward than forward. For a reason she didn't understand this roof morphed into another one. Visions of an incident she hadn't thought about in years played in her mind like a movie from her childhood.

Her friend Janie came to play and climbed on the neighbor's roof by scaling an oak tree growing nearby. Ruthie couldn't resist joining her. She loved walking around looking down at the yard, the street, and people passing by until Mom darted out of the house and demanded she and Janie get down. She yearned to see Mom, but first she had to get out of these woods.

She crawled, stopped, then repeated the action until finally she reached the edge of the shed. The six inches between the roof of the house and the storage unit loomed large. Where was Thad? "Now, I have to step over thin air. That's worse than a high-wire act. At least they have a tightrope." She hollered to Thad, even though she couldn't see him.

He let out a loud sigh. "Honestly," he mumbled, but louder he said, "Stay where you are. I'm moving the ladder so I can help you get from the shed's roof to the window, which I left open, by the way."

In a few minutes, Thad appeared from the waist up at the roof's edge. She grasped his hand so tight her knuckles turned white. After she stood to take the stride over the space, weakness swept through her like it did when she had the flu. She couldn't do it. But she had to. Tears built inside and flooded her with her own cowardice and worthlessness. Going in the window was such a small thing after all they'd been through. If only she wasn't afraid of heights. If only that Ferris wheel hadn't stopped with her and Mom at the top.

She sucked in three deep breaths, squeezed her eyes tight, and pretended she would step over a puddle of water. As she took a big stride forward, her pulse pounded in her temples.

Whew! She landed on snow on the roofing. As she lay down, relief rushed through her veins like Niagara Falls. She grabbed the top window jamb and pushed her legs inside.

"Are you at the window?"

Tilted, she sat wedged between the side jamb and one side of the faucet. Wiggling, she tried to push over the sink, but she fit too tight. It had taken every nerve she had to walk over thin air. Now this. She couldn't think straight.

"Are you okay?"

Sure, Thad! She inhaled and exhaled to keep from

jumping out of her skin.

"Are you alright?" He repeated.

She swallowed the nausea in her throat and forced a steady tone. "Yes, I'm fine. Give me a minute." She wasn't sure she could finish the job in sixty seconds, but she'd bought time to gather herself.

A brief silence followed, then Thad said, "You got it, but just one. We need to get inside that house."

Pressure. The last thing she needed. She positioned her left leg on the other side of the faucet and straddled it.

"Could you please let me know you're alright?"

She considered her awkward position high above the floor. Her head swam. She clasped her hands around the jambs.

"By the way, you're a natural gymnast, but be careful. Don't hurt yourself getting to the floor."

Rising six inches to clear the faucet, she pushed her body, twitching and quivering, over the sink to the edge of the counter. Maybe the memory of her childhood adventure on the roof had been divine intervention. God had been with her all along. She couldn't have made it across the roof by herself. "Thank you," she said before she jumped down.

She rubbed her arms to stop the irritation scraping her skin like a dish scrubber over the entire incident. Neither Thad nor Moose realized the emotional trauma they'd put her through. It would do no good to complain. They wouldn't understand how horrified she'd been.

"You're awfully quiet. I don't see you. Are you okay? Are you inside now?"

"I'm fine. I'm inside."

"Okay, I'll join Moose on the porch."

She needed compensation for the agony she'd endured. The best place to sleep in the entire building? Nah. Moose should have that after all he'd been through. She would never take extra food. There had to be something though. Aha. She had it.

Knocking resounded on the front door.

"It's nice in here. There's a refrigerator and stove, plus a couple of sofas. I think there's a bathroom down this little hall."

Loud banging pounded the front door. "Let us in."

Ruthie clapped as an impish nature rose inside her. "You don't want to come through the window?"

"Ruuuthie."

"Yes, Moose."

"Let us in."

"You want to come in the house to get out of the cold now?"

"Right now! This is not funny."

"Ah, let me see." This was more fun than she could have imagined. Moose was right though. He'd done so much to take care of them she shouldn't joke with him about their safety or comfort, or lose control of her senses.

"Ruuthie. Now."

It wasn't Moose and Thad's fault she was the only one who fit through the window. Had Thad tried hard enough? She sighed. She'd take him at his word. She let her eyes move over her body. She was fine. Everyone was fine. That's what mattered.

"Ruuuthie."

She held out her hands. They weren't shaking anymore. "I'm coming," she said in her sweetest tone before she swung open the door.

"Why you." Disbelief lined Moose's tone. He turned toward Thad. "What do you think? Should we share the food you packed with her?"

Thad shot Ruthie a rascally look. "We'll see."

Moose picked up his and Ruhtie's bags and walked in, Thad right behind him.

"Hmm, pretty nice for such a desolate location," Thad said. Then, he jumped up and down. "There's a thermostat on the wall. It reads sixty-three." His voice rose several octaves. "Can I turn it up?"

"I'm warm." Ruthie fanned herself.

"You'll cool off when you settle down from breaking in." Thad snickered.

If he only knew.

"I wouldn't want to increase their bill." Moose scrunched his nose. He probably wanted to say "yes," but thought no. "Maybe we could go to sixty-eight. We won't use it for long. We'll turn it down when we leave." He laid two twenty-dollar bills on a small table at the entryway. "Our rental fee for the night." He rubbed his palms together. "We must've entered a large country kitchen. This living area has two sofas and several easy chairs, plus a dining table and chairs. Decide who wants what? I'm tired."

Ruthie placed the to-go sandwiches in the refrigerator and turned around. "Anything's fine with me."

Thad wandered down the short hall and returned. "There's a room back there with a daybed. If you two want to bunk in here, I'll take it."

Moose waved toward the rear of the house. "Sure, go ahead. Any soft spot sounds good to me."

Ruthie reached in Moose's football bag, pulled out a blanket, and handed it to him.

He wrapped it around his body, propped a cushion on the sofa's armrest, then plopped down on it. When he stretched out, his feet dangled over the side. Ruthie picked them up and placed them across the arm of the couch at the other end.

"What about a watch?" Thad glanced at Moose. "I'm the night owl, remember? I'll take the first one." He pointed toward Ruthie. "Second?"

"Sure." The journey here and the daring act on the rooftops had sapped all of Ruthie's energy, but they all had to do their parts. She motioned toward Moose. "Last night, he took the second shift. Even though he was supposed to crash for another three hours, he joined me in the kitchen fairly early." Ruthie looked down at him. "Poor guy."

"Ah, he's okay. If I didn't know better, I'd think the two of you had a thing going."

"Me with Moose, a football coach?"

Thad stretched. "Yeah, you, but we're taking up your sack time. Rest. Lie down and sleep. I'll stay alert."

Thad left. Then Ruthie spread out a blanket, thanked God she was indoors out of the brutal weather, and collapsed on the other sofa.

Moose waved at her. "Hey you."

"Yes."

"Do you think a grammarian and a football coach could spend days on end talking to each other?"

What an odd question. Wait. Did he mean what her exhausted brain thought? Date? Not just casual dating? Did he mean a serious relationship? Her skin tingled.

"Sure, why not as long as the football coach explained that first down thing?"

"Good."

Ruthie pulled her blanket close around her heart. Her eyelids grew heavy. If only Hucklesford would leave them alone long enough to get a good night's sleep.

Chapter Twenty-Two

Someone touched Ruthie's arm. She awakened with a start. Tried to remember where she was. Why were she and Moose on couches in a large country kitchen?

Thad stood over her.

Ah, the building she had broken into in the park. "Hi Thad, my turn? Anything suspicious?"

Thad yawned. "Not so far. Get me up at nine unless something happens."

Ruthie gave him a thumbs up. "Will do."

When Thad left, Ruthie forced her body off of the sofa, walked to the kitchen, and sat down at the table. Moonglow shone through the same window she'd crawled in. Had she really broken into a public structure? Even though it seemed surreal, she'd done it. She'd also slept outside in the cold too many nights. Tired of running, she slumped in her seat. "No more."

An hour passed without a sound breaking the silence inside or outdoors. As Ruthie's tense muscles loosened, she rummaged in her bag for something to eat for breakfast. She'd packed items so quickly she'd forgotten she included coffee. Seeing it, she rushed to the cabinet to find a coffee maker and cups.

Within thirty minutes, a vanilla bean aroma wafted over the room. She poured a cup of coffee and sipped. The drink warmed her the way only a fresh cup of coffee could. Hoping an evil noise wouldn't invade her peace, she pressed her hands around the cup.

Moose stirred and sat up. "Can I have some of that?"

Ruthie gave him her best grin. "Of course." She fixed him a cup. "Here ya' go."

Moose took a swallow. "Delicious." He set down the drink on the end table by the sofa and rubbed his arm. "In my wildest imagination, I never dreamed something like this could happen. There are moments when I can't believe it's real. If we can hold on through the day, by tonight we should find help and safety."

Moose spoke encouraging words, even though his jaw sagged like a basset hound. He blew out a puff of air. "The only good thing out of this disaster is meeting you."

"Ahh, that's so nice." Certain now she'd read the right meaning into Moose's words last night about a grammarian and a football coach, Ruthie's pulse sped up. She cared more about Moose than she ever had any other guy, but she didn't understand her emotions.

Maybe she didn't want to understand them. For as long as she could remember until now, her life fit into a plan which gave her financial security. Caring about Moose would distract from her career. She couldn't have that, could she? Wait. Did her professorship mean the world to her, or did it mean the world to Mom and Dad?

She loved her parents. They wanted the best for

her, but surely the goals they set for her included happiness. After all, Mom and Dad married.

"You need to get your nose out of those books and experience life. Stop reading about it and live it." Moose picked up his coffee and took another sip.

The nerve of him. He could've slapped her and not shocked her more. He was right though. Kinda' scary, he knew her so well. "Maybe I will. How about you? Do you need to get off of the football field and see what else the world offers?"

Moose's neck turned tomato red. It appeared he tried to laugh, but the sound left his mouth as a soft snort. "Touché. I'm guilty of....of....what's that psychological term? Uh, projection. I'm like the teapot accusing the coffee carafe of taking up too much room on the counter." Moose looked at Ruthie with sheepish eyes. "Maybe we could explore the great beyond together."

Ruthie smiled at his words, even the ones about the teapot and coffee carafe. Maybe he was right. Perhaps neither of them had met the person who made them want to step off of the counter. "Let's try—a teapot and a coffee carafe wandering through life kinda' like characters in Alice in Wonderland."

Moose chuckled, then took her hand. "It's settled. We'll start with dinner at my house and a football game since I already asked. Next, we'll go to a play, or whatever English professors like to do."

Thad entered. "You're up."

"Excellent observation and on a minimal amount of sleep."

They all laughed at Moose's joke.

"Join us for a cup of coffee. We might as well have

it with the pimento cheese sandwiches," Ruthie said.

They finished the coffee and sandwiches, packed their bags, and left.

Thad eyed Moose for several moments. "Were you serious about a job for me at the college?"

Moose cocked an eyebrow. "Of course, once we're safe, I'll have a brief visit with my mom and dad, then return to school."

"I never wanted to come here this winter. With a lunatic roaming around the hills, I sure don't want to stay. If you'd like to know the truth, I resent Dad doing this to me just because I'm not a computer guru."

Moose stopped walking and Thad and Ruthie did too. As the three of them bunched together, Moose said, "If you think your dad wronged you, then you have to forgive him."

Thad shrugged. "He's the dad. I'm the kid. I have to do what he says."

Thad's words shot through Ruthie like an arrow. She stumbled. "None of us are perfect." She righted herself and said, "We all make mistakes in our relationships with others. We all need forgiveness. If Christ can forgive us for our sins, plus forgiving those who tortured and killed him, we can forgive each other."

"I never considered that." Thad directed his gaze to Moose. "Did you forgive your dad for needling you about becoming a colonel in the Army?"

"Yes, it wasn't easy. I had to pray about it, but I did it. If I hadn't, I'm not sure I could've become a football coach. I had to free myself of bitterness before I could claim the life I believed God wanted for me."

"Why do you think God chose you to play football

and coach?"

"Who else would've given me a passion for it along with the talent to do it? Don't get me wrong. I'm not one of the greats. I'm using my gift to the best of my ability."

"Uh-huh." Thad drew out the words. "I get it. You don't have to be the greatest to succeed."

Moose nodded.

"Has your dad accepted your choice?"

Moose focused into the distance. "I think he has. Hmph. Probably reluctantly, but yes, we're okay now."

Thad directed his gaze to Ruthie. "How about you?"

"Even though I would've liked more of a social life, I love my mom and dad dearly. They've done so many good things for me. I can't wait to call them."

Moose motioned forward. "On to the truck."

In fifteen minutes, they reached the vehicle, its tires slashed and as useless as deflated footballs.

Chapter Twenty-Three

Pain shot through Ruthie for Thad when she looked at the damaged tires on his truck, making it impossible to drive it from the icy parking lot in the park.

He grabbed his waist, bent double, and plopped down on the ice-cold earth. "Noooo." He wailed.

Ruthie touched Moose's arm. "I'm surprised he didn't shoot out the windows," she whispered.

Thad rubbed the heel of his palm against his chest. "He probably didn't want us to hear the shots. We might've left if we had. More than likely, he wanted to keep us right where we were until daylight, when he could see better. My two cents' worth, he's hiding, lurking, waiting to shoot us."

Moose squatted down next to him. "Don't worry. I'll arrange to have the truck towed and buy new tires for it as soon as we get to civilization."

Thad and Moose stood. Then Thad said, "I don't think we're going to make it."

"Of course we will." Ruthie hugged him.

Moose gave Thad a man hug. Afterward, Moose

must've stiffened his backbone as far as it would go, because he looked several inches taller. "We will leave these woods."

A whizzing sound pierced the air. Frozen snow cracked and shattered as a bullet hit beside Moose's boot. He jumped; his eyes wide.

Thad clapped his hands over his ears. "Nooo," he moaned.

Ruthie struggled to stay upright as her knees buckled.

Moose snatched the bags. "Run."

Ruthie prayed under her breath as she fled up the mountain into the forest. "Lord, I'm so tired. Give me the strength I need." Finding a force within, she grabbed Thad's arm, pulling him along, racing to nowhere.

Thad broke her hold. "I can't do it."

"Yes, you can." She looked to the right. Then to the left. Where could they hide? Running. Running. Running to where?

Moose stopped without warning. She bumped into him as he turned toward Thad. "Help me move this boulder."

One of the biggest rocks Ruthie had ever seen lay to the right of their path.

Thad jumped to attention, then hurried to stand at one end of the rock. Moose pulled at the other end as Thad pushed.

Jogging in place, Ruthie watched. The boulder didn't budge. She left and combed the area for an oak limb. Yes. She found one and dragged it to Moose and Thad. With shaking hands, she placed it in an indention underneath the boulder. Using the branch as a lever, she pressed down. Moose pulled. Thad pushed. The stone rolled and landed in the middle of the pathway, covering the trail. Perfect.

"Let's go." Moose and Thad snatched up the bags.

The three of them raced to their right.

Crack. Crack. Crack.

Panting, Moose turned his head and looked behind him. "He'll have to stop soon to go around the barricade we left for him. Does anybody see a place to hide?"

"N-n-n. No." Thad sputtered.

"No." Ruthie had to push her body hard to keep pace with Moose.

Thad caught up to Moose. "Should we stop, get out the rifle, and fire at him?"

"I'd rather find a safe spot."

"The only thing, there isn't one."

"We'll see one. Keep looking."

Ruthie gasped for air. "I'm so tired of snow, but I'm praying for snow now to cover our tracks."

A few minutes after Ruthie's comment, flakes fell from the sky.

Thad caught one in his hand. "Looks like God answered…" Disbelief washed over Thad's face as he ran next to Ruthie. "…your prayer?"

"Snow and more. Look how the freezing weather stopped the water cascading over that large slab of granite. It will make a roof for us." Ruthie pointed to their right. "Moose taught me that. We've already stayed at a waterfall."

"Head for it." Moose made a sharp turn.

After forcing her tight leg muscles and hurt ankle to keep up with Moose and Thad, Ruthie turned and checked for footprints. "Yes." She pumped her arm. "The snow covered our tracks." Optimism rose inside her like smoke from one of her and Moose's fires. "Hucklesford will not find us here."

Moose looked behind them. "I hope you're right." Then, he turned and glanced down. "You two watch your step. There's a fallen tree."

Ruthie ran around it, its barren branches spread on the snow-covered earth, its glory uprooted by the storm.

Moose and Thad set down the bags beside a creek. Stilled splashes shot up from stones where falling water cascaded over the edge of the boulder from the waterfall into the stream, every drop frozen in time, glistening like diamonds in the sun.

Moose put up his thumb in a salute. "This works. You two go ahead. I'll get the bags."

Ruthie and Thad went to the waterfall, walked underneath their granite roof covered in static water, and entered the area behind it. "It's perfect." Ruthie rubbed part of the icy rock with her gloved hand. "These stones sticking out on the sides of the waterfall will help break up the wind. We can see outside, but this high, wide icy cascade covers us well. When Hucklesford comes along, he won't see us. We'll watch him go right past here." Ruthie shrugged. "Well, we can easily place a fortress on the trail we took to get here. He couldn't climb up the other side."

Thad gave her a high-five.

After Moose joined them, he leaned down, took a peek, and whistled. "Just what we need." He glanced at Ruthie. "I'll take in the bags, then we can look for twigs and rocks to put a barrier."

After they set up their campsite, they hurried into

the woods. Moose wandered to the left while Thad went straight. Ruthie searched the right side of the forest like a bloodhound on a scent.

She spied the perfect foundation for a barricade. A thin layer of ice covered a two-foot-by-four-foot boulder with small ruts. Studying the large stone, she realized she couldn't move it. In frustration, she kicked the ice beside her prize, walking back to the waterfall with kindling. She put her hands on her hips. "I spotted a great base for our barricade, but it's too big to move."

Moose snapped to attention. "Show us. We'll figure out something."

Taking only five minutes, the three of them reached the proposed obstruction.

Moose squatted down and assessed the stone. "If we can upend this thing, we can roll it to the trail."

"I never considered that," Ruthie said.

Moose stood and brushed off his hands. "While we figure out the best way to move it, see if you can find a branch to use as a lever."

"Right away." Ruthie pivoted and left.

Taking a slow stroll, stopping every foot or so, she scrutinized the area in front of her, then right, then left. Someone could've swept the forest floor and it wouldn't have been any cleaner.

She trudged past twigs and underbrush, seeing nothing large enough to use as a lever. It seemed she'd walked forever. She would not return to Moose and Thad empty handed though. Keeping her gaze glued to the ground, she continued for what seemed like miles without finding what they needed. Finally growing tired, she stopped to catch her breath.

Did she miss something on the way? Looking

around, she spotted a clump of pine trees. How odd, she hadn't noticed them on her way here. She placed her hand over her mouth and spun in circles as she searched the forest for a landmark she would remember. Weakness swept through her.

Lost, she would freeze—alone.

~

Still squatting beside the boulder, Moose rubbed his hand over his forehead. "Finally, I figured out the perfect spot to place the stone and how to aim it to get it there." He turned to see if Thad paid attention. He did. "We can put the lever right there." He pointed to an area where the trail grew narrow, stood, and brushed off his hands. "We'll need to dig through the snow and ice then make an indention in the ground." He stiffened as though someone poked him. "Speaking of the lever..." He glanced at his watch and his gut wrenched. "Ruthie left an hour ago. Where is she?"

Thad snapped to attention like a soldier. "I don't know."

"She's missing." In the scourge of winter, Moose started sweating.

Thad grabbed Moose's arm. "Oh no, bu-bu-but, don't worry. We'll find her. I'm not too great at lots of things. I'm good at locating things, people, and pets." Thad nodded. "I am, really. I always found our kitten when she hid. The time old Rouser didn't come home for a week..." Thad's words grew weaker until they drifted into nothingness.

Moose's brain froze as solid as the earth beneath him. "I don't know which way to go. She'll freeze out there."

"Nah, man, she's not going to freeze 'cause we'll

find her." Thad tugged on Moose's arm. "Come on."

Thad was right. They would rescue Ruthie. There were so many trees, but they had no leaves. Except for the snow and fog, he and Thad could see fine. Who was he kidding? Nothing lay before him except a white world, where most of the trees looked like skinny ghosts, the earth getting deeper in snow by the second. He watched flakes fall to the right and left of him. If he called out Ruthie's name, Hucklesford might shoot all of them. He clenched his hands into fists and dug his fingernails into his palms.

The flashlight. Even in the daylight, if he swirled it and turned it off and on, Ruthie would recognize the beams. "Thad, I forgot something. I'm going to the campsite."

Thad held up. "Hey man, you're just upset. Everything's going to be fine. Don't run off."

"I have to." Moose marched in place.

"Uh, okay. We need a marker, so we'll know where to meet in case I find her while you're gone."

"Yeah, you're right, but what?"

Thad put his hand over his forehead and peered into the distance.

Unable to stand still, Moose bounced his foot. "Hurry. Get something."

Thad waved his hand as though he tried to swish away Moose's anxiety. "I will. Calm down. Be cool. I promise. We'll find her." He walked off. In a few moments, he returned, his arms engulfing small and medium-sized stones. "I'll make a pile right here and you'll know..."

"I got it."

Chapter Twenty-Four

Moose moved as fast as his feet would take him through the snow. With his shoes sliding on the frosty surface, he waved his arms to keep his balance. How could he have forgotten the flashlight? It had been thirty minutes already since they realized Ruthie was missing. He was wasting precious time. *Oh, dear Lord, please help me find Ruthie. Please keep her safe.*

Finally, he reached their campsite. Snatching the flashlight from his bag, he rushed out, following the direction Ruthie had taken, swinging the light in swooping motions. Shaken to the bone, he moved the light in bigger circles to keep it shining through the thick, white curtain closing in on the forest.

He bit his tongue to keep from calling out Ruthie's name. Panting, he trudged like a madman, stumbling, skating over the snow, jerking his gaze right, then left. At last, he spotted Thad's pile of stones. If only Ruthie would look for them. If only their cell phones worked. If only...if only...Moose gasped for air.

He bent double and tried to breathe while every muscle in his body twisted. Finally, he straightened and slowed his pace. It wouldn't do anyone any good if he couldn't go on. Ruthie probably tried to stay in a straight line so she could backtrack. What if she grew disoriented and wandered off of her path? Would she have veered to the left or the right? It would take a miracle to find Ruthie in these woods. Moose clutched the flashlight like he would a lifeline. Suddenly, he bumped into someone. Ruthie. Oh please, yes. In an instant, his brain flip-flopped. Hucklesford. *Heaven help us all.*

Thad.

Moose let out a loud sigh of relief Thad wasn't Hucklesford. Then he went limp inside because Thad wasn't Ruthie.

"Ruthie's on the left side." Thad waved his hand in that direction.

"How do you know that?" Moose's frantic voice drifted into the wind.

Thad wiped snowflakes off of his nose and gave Moose a harsh stare. "I told you. I'm good at this. Following a direct path from the boulder as far as Ruthie could've gone in an hour I veered to the right. I just started back on the other side." Thad pointed to their left. "She's over there."

"All right, at least you have an idea. I'm out of them." Moose motioned for Thad to lead the way.

Thad scanned the landscape with steady eyes. The intense look sent a spark of hope over Moose. He couldn't recall a time he'd needed help as much as he did now. His dad had instilled the importance of toughness and independence at all costs. He'd told Moose, "Always remember. No one cares about you. You're on your own." Right now, those words carried no more weight than tissue paper.

His dad had not counted on Ruthie getting lost in a snowstorm. If Moose could have, he would've contacted the National Guard. Gratitude like he'd never known filled him for Thad's help and encouragement. Holding in tears, he blinked several times.

Thad took hold of Moose's arm. "Hey man, look." He pointed to their left. "There she is. See."

Moose charged to her, stumbling on the way. He grabbed her and hugged her as tight as he could without squeezing the air out of her. So much joy filled his heart it was a wonder it didn't jump out of his chest. "I'm so glad to see you." It was all he could do to keep the welled-up tears choking him at bay. He didn't know if Ruthie cared about him or not, but Dad was wrong. People cared about other people. He cared from the depths of his soul about Ruthie."

Thad grinned so big it was a wonder his cheeks didn't tear. "I told you we'd find her."

Moose gave Thad a man hug. "Yes, you did. Thank you." Dad was really wrong.

"I can't believe you found me. I can't believe you found me." Ruthie spoke between sobs.

Thad rushed over. "You can't go running off like that again."

Ruthie crumpled against his chest.

Thad gave her a loose hug, then held her out from him. "We got you."

She reached out and tapped Thad's arm, then Moose's. "You're really here."

Moose was glad Thad was talking to Ruthie. If he said anything right now, he couldn't hold in the tears rushing to his eyes.

Thad put his hands on his hips. "Of course, we're here. You didn't think we'd leave you, did you? What would we do without you? We can't cook and find places to hide all by ourselves."

Ruthie blinked.

Moose tried to speak, but the words stuck on the emotion knotted in his throat.

Thad relaxed his stance. "We're not letting you out of our sight again. Okay?"

Ruthie met Thad's gaze, then looked at Moose as though she still couldn't believe they were here. "Okay."

"Well, where's the lever?"

Ruthie sighed.

Thad chuckled.

She looked at him and laughed loud.

Moose joined them.

"Unfortunately, I don't have one. I stayed zoned in looking for one, forgetting about everything except the lever, because I wanted to make it as difficult as possible for Hucklesford to sneak up on us. The farther I walked without finding a branch to upend the stone, the more upset I got. When I started to search on my way back to the campsite, I saw pine trees I hadn't noticed before. I knew I was lost."

"Not anymore. We found you." Kindness lined Thad's words. "We should move that boulder, though."

"Right. Both of you stay put. You can come get me if I go too far away." Moose meandered into the fog and snowflakes.

Within fifteen minutes, he dragged a thick branch to Thad and Ruthie. "Let's go."

~

Ruthie blinked when she saw the limb. "How did I miss that?"

"You didn't. It was a bit to the right of your path," Moose said.

Ruthie sprang on her toes and clapped. "Thank goodness you have it." She wanted to tell Moose and Thad how their devotion to find her had touched her heart. She sucked air through her nose, then exhaled. English teachers always had words, didn't they? Sure they did. She just couldn't find them right now. "Thank you for searching for me."

Thad's head jerked back.

Moose's mouth gaped.

"We would've looked day and night until we found you," Thad said.

Moose pointed up. "I thought it would take a miracle to find you. And, that's what we got. Praise God."

"Amen," Thad said.

Even though Ruthie hadn't seen it until she wandered alone with no way out of this desolate forest, Thad and Moose's steadfast loyalty had been with her all along. Sharing life's hardships with someone she could count on lifted her above the agony.

Moose shot an affectionate look at Ruthie.

Between Thad's words and Moose's expression, she experienced so much warmth she checked to see if the icicles melted on the tree above her.

Then the three of them walked to the stone— together. Moose and Thad dug the indention and placed the lever. Then, he and Thad tugged and pulled on the sides while Ruthie used the large branch to thrust the rock upward. Finally, ice cracking resounded in the forest. Ruthie straightened and swiped her brow. Thad and Moose got on the same side of the large boulder and rolled it to the narrow spot on the pathway to the waterfall.

Moose gave it the once over. "It's ideal."

They completed their fortification and Ruthie turned toward Thad. "It's twilight. According to my tummy, it's time to eat. Let's pool our resources."

"You bet."

They walked to the campsite, where they'd left their bags. Thad rummaged through his stash until he pulled out a box of wafers, then a jar. "I love peanut butter crackers."

"Way to go." Ruthie gave him a high-five. "I have..." She reached in her bag and got out a cellophane wrapped box. "Protein bars." She stuffed them back into her satchel. "We'll eat those for breakfast. Let's see. Thanks to Thad's hospitality, I have three thermoses of coffee, a bag of chips, and a can of tuna." She pulled out a can opener and held it up. "I brought this too."

"Hey…hey, we're in good shape." Thad's words rolled out with a chuckle.

Moose and Thad built a fire while Ruthie spread out their dinner. After they sat down, she poured cups of coffee, then held up a plastic spoon. "I gave each of us a paper plate, also courtesy of Thad. Dig into the tuna. It's good with potato chips."

Moose tried it. "Hmm. Not bad." He sipped his coffee. "Ah, but this…this warms the soul."

Thad nodded.

Ruthie took several bites of her tuna, then munched a chip. "It's a robust meal."

"Umm. Yes." Thad stuffed in a whole chip. "I'm glad you packed this."

Ruthie smiled. "Look what I have for dessert." She held up a package of cookies. "They have chocolate chips."

"Hmm. Hmm." Thad gulped down the rest of his meal.

Ruthie handed him the cookies. He took three. Then Moose ate the last of his tuna and reached for one. Ruthie directed her gaze to Thad. "Moose and I went without actual meals until we reached your place. Thank goodness for you."

Thad flashed a toothy smile.

"I agree." Moose set down his paper plate, leaned against a boulder, stretched out, and munched on the cookie.

Ruthie peeked through the motionless cascade. "Look outside at the pile of snow. If it gets too high and freezes..."

"What about oxygen?" A tremor lined Thad's voice.

"We'll have air because the precipitation lands in front and on the sides of the waterfall." Moose pointed at the natural ice sculpture in front of them. "Look, there's no snow in the spaces between the icicles."

"Okay. I see that now," Thad said.

Ruthie ate a cookie, then surveyed their campsite. What if she had been wrong when she said Hucklesford would go right past this place? "Let's move the debris blocking the pathway closer. If Hucklesford does spot this place, if he's brave enough to challenge the landscape, he could go around our fortification without us hearing him with so much snow on the ground."

"Yes." Thad sprang up. "If we put the barricade closer to the fire, maybe the boulder won't freeze, and we can get past it if we need to." He moaned. "But the snow could block our way out."

"We have plenty of matches for melting and rocks for pommeling ice or frozen snow. You both make good points. Since it's at least ten feet from where we're sitting to the top of the granite slab above us, we could construct a scree. Believe me, if he broke through it, we'd hear him. Loosening the stones in one of those things creates chaos. I speak from personal experience."

"Unfortunately, he does," Ruthie added before they walked to their pathway barricade.

Moose and Thad moved the boulder to lay beside the waterfall while Ruthie carried the branches to their campsite.

Moose pulled two plastic bags from his football gear. "Thad and I will gather more firewood and material for the scree slope." Moose turned to Ruthie. "You stay here and build our fortress. Unfortunately, you know what a rockslide looks like up-close."

"Right. I'm glad to do that. I'm in no hurry to lose my way again." What if they got lost? She couldn't bear it. "Come to think of it, maybe the two of you should stay close," she called out as they walked away.

Remembering the gut-wrenching aloneness shrouding her in the forest only a few hours ago, Ruthie twisted a strand of hair so tight it hurt. If only she could see a trace of them. She rushed to the entrance to their hideout. The snow obstructed her view. *Come back. Come back.* She blinked to keep from crying. She would not do it, not now, not after all that had happened.

Since the wreck on Friday, survival had taken charge of every waking minute. Things that once meant so much meant little to nothing. The PhD Mom and Dad had required her to earn had served its purpose, but with society's goods and services swept away, it wasn't worth much. She'd had fun Christmas shopping for her family, but now it seemed she'd done it in a different life, a life where she concocted a special blend of coffee for herself every morning. Now she couldn't remember the taste of the morning pick-me-up. Her students formed the thin thread still connecting her to the world she left behind. She would hold tight to her memories of them.

If she, Moose, and Thad didn't get out of these woods, her Christmas would take place only in her soul. She peered into the snowflakes to see more snowflakes. She sank down on the blanket.

"Hey, what you doin' down there?"

"I'm so glad to see you." Ruthie hopped up, skidded, and bumped into Thad.

He dropped his bag of sticks and righted her before he squeezed her arm. "Yeah, I know. We're going get this place Hucklesford proof. Then we're going to relax."

Thankful for Thad's friendship and the encouragement, Ruthie smiled. "Right."

In minutes, Moose joined them, dropped his branches, and brushed off his gloves. "That ought to keep you busy for a while. It looks as though we'll need a couple more loads of firewood and rocks. If we had a wheelbarrow…" He sighed. "We don't."

Moose and Thad left. Ruthie rushed to the entryway, where she watched for as long as she could see them. Twilight would turn to night. Who knew what that would bring?

Chapter Twenty-Five

Ruthie scrutinized the boulder she needed to use as a foundation for the scree she aspired to build. Could she construct a masterpiece? If so, would Hucklesford accept it as real and walk away from their campsite? Her insides quivered. She was an advanced grammar professor, who knew nothing about screes, except for the one Moose slid down. Remembering the accident, she couldn't keep tears from forming. She never wanted to see another scree, let alone build one.

She slumped to the ground. Her mother's voice called out to her in a whisper from faraway. "What? What are you saying, Mother?"

"When all seems hopeless…"

"Yes."

"When all seems hopeless…"

"Yes."

"Think of your blessings."

That was it.

"Okay, Mother."

Moose knows how to survive. Thad knows how to get to the highway. God has taken care of us ever since the wreck, supplying us with food and shelter. We have warm clothes and blankets. Barring a few scratches and bruises, we're all fine. Thank you, Lord. Please give me courage to start on the fake rockslide. In Jesus' name I pray. Amen.

She stood, her vision still a little skewed from staring at the boulder. She picked up a branch and scraped snow off of it. After the top of the foundation came into focus, she inspected it. She could do it.

Using the larger stones, she built the wall part of the way up on the right side, eyed it, and calculated the trajectory of objects if they were to fall. To make her rockslide appear authentic, she placed some of the stones on the ground in strategic spots where they would've landed if they'd rolled off of the scree. Trying to create perfection, she grew tense and tightened her muscles, already aching from the cold.

Contempt for Hucklesford moved over her like heavy fog. How dare he force them to take drastic measures when they'd done nothing to him. Before she knew it, anger boiled inside her like an overheated stew, but the steam didn't escape like it did from a pot. It burned in her throat.

"We're here with another delivery."

Moose's voice shot through the angst, reminding her she had a friend and brought a sweet sensation. He and Thad dumped their resources in a pile, then hugged her. Moose shined the flashlight on her handiwork and gave her an approving nod. "Not bad."

"Thank you. I'm doing my best." Ruthie forced an optimistic tone into her voice.

"Man, let's get this done. I'm ready to sit down by the fire. It's freezing out there." Thad rubbed his arms.

Ruthie's scalp prickled as she watched them disappear, but she shot to her task and added more rocks to the scree. "One more night, just one more night," she mumbled over and over while she worked on the fortress. After thirty minutes of bending over, picking up rocks, and arranging them, she stretched. Her body cried out for rest, but Thad and Moose arrived with more material.

Moose peeked at her creation. "Lookin' good."

He and Thad dropped more sticks and rocks and left. They each needed to do their part to stay alive. She moaned and forced herself to return to work. After thirty minutes, she assessed her rockslide. Even though her scree wasn't as high as the one Moose tumbled down, it resembled it.

Exhausted, she sank to the ground with a few leftover rocks in her lap. They were close to civilization. If they survived tonight and escaped Hucklesford, they would find help.

Moose and Thad returned and dumped more material for the faux scree. Then they pitched in to help. Moose added stone at the top, where she hadn't been able to reach, to make the faux scree higher.

Ruthie moved her hands faster, the load lighter. With three of them working, in no time they finished her design plus Moose's contribution to the size of it.

He scanned the creation, then gave Thad a light slap on his back. "Let's rest."

As soon as Thad sat down on the blanket, he motioned toward Ruthie's bag. "English professor, do you have any books in there?"

"Of course, I do."

"What kinds of things are in them?"

Ruthie couldn't resist. "Nouns, verbs, prepositions, adverbs, adjectives, those sorts of things." She flashed

Thad a mischievous grin.

He swatted the air as though he waved away her words. "I mean the stories. I might read one if you have something interesting."

"I know. I was teasing." She pulled out a novel and held it up. "Ah, a classic. This is *An American Tragedy* by Theodore Dreiser. Moose gave a speech on it once."

"Uh, yeah, it was required to pass a course I had to take in college. I don't like public speaking unless I'm talking football."

"I get it, man, but I can't play or watch a game in here and I want something to do." Thad directed his gaze to Ruthie. "So, tell me about the book."

"Dreiser based the main character on a convicted criminal who took a woman for a boat ride on a lake, beat her with a tennis racquet, and left her to drown."

Thad puckered his mouth. "That sounds gruesome."

"It's long, an older book too, but it drew lots of attention in its day." Ruthie turned her thoughts to literature and forgot she propped up on frosted granite.

"What do you like about it?"

"It shows how life's hardships and temptation can cause someone to betray what they know is right. It also illustrates the sadness doing so can cause. The main character grew up poor and grabbed the wrong ticket out of poverty. To better his financial and social standings, he faced an ethical and spiritual decision. He committed a crime."

Thad pulled his eyebrows low. "What else do you have in there?"

"A little too grim, huh?"

"Exactly. Maybe another time. I need something

light right now."

"Let's see." Ruthie rummaged in the bag and held up another book. *Ripley's Believe It or Not.* She passed it to Thad. "Here ya' go."

He opened it and started reading. "Hey, did you know fish can get seasick?"

"Sounds like you're already hooked, no pun intended." Ruthie chuckled.

Thad read to himself for several seconds. "It says right here when someone created artificial storm waves in a glass bowl, the goldfish in there got seasick."

Ruthie gave him a thumbs up. "I'm happy you found something." Reading would keep him from worrying about the weather and Hucklesford.

He stuck his nose in the book.

Ruthie's eyelids closed as though they were shades someone pulled down. As soon as she jerked up, the phenomenon repeated.

Finally, Moose put his hand on her arm. "Thad seems entertained as much as possible under the circumstances. Let's get some sleep."

"Sounds good to me."

Thad looked up from the book. "You two go to sleep. I'll read until three o'clock, then I'll get wake up..." He glanced at Moose, then Ruthie. "Which one of you?"

Moose raised his hand. "Me. I'll light a fire before I go to sleep. If you hear footsteps outside, or someone walking outside our camp, put out the fire immediately and wake me. Otherwise, get me up at three as planned."

"You bet."

"Be sure to watch it closely."

"I will."

Moose built the fire, and they settled in for the night.

Ruthie fell asleep as soon as she lay down.

When Moose woke her the next morning at six o'clock, Thad lay in a sleeping bag near the rear of the waterfall. "Thad's resting peacefully. You do the same."

She hopped up and Moose stretched out on the blanket.

Ruthie propped up against the slab of granite at the rear of their campsite and opened a book about World War II the history professor at Hilltop College loaned her. She was glad Moose had saved it in case…She didn't want to think of her car at the bottom of the cliff, Hucklesford, or how cold she was. She intended to take advantage of this morning, so quiet she could hear a bird's wings flutter.

After she read fifteen chapters, she glanced at her watch. It was time to wake Moose and find breakfast for everyone. They'd had a restful night without any interference from Hucklesford. Soon they would leave this forsaken forest. After searching in her bag for a few minutes, she pulled protein bars out of it, but when she looked at them, she imagined pancakes oozing with butter and syrup.

She wandered to Moose and gently patted his wrist.

"Huh? What? What is it?" He rubbed his eyelids. "Oh, hi."

"Hello. Time to get up and get moving." She gave two bars to Moose. "Take one to Thad."

Ice cracked in the distance.

Ruthie jumped. "What was that?"

Moose stiffened. "I didn't hear or see anyone last night, so I let the fire burn. Did you put it out?"

Ruthie slapped her cheek. "N-No. Maybe we heard a catamount, or a deer." She peeked out of a space between the icicles. Red and yellow colors shined like a neon sign.

Moose sprang up and broke off pieces of ice, throwing them over the smoldering fire.

Ruthie joined him, dropping icicles onto the dying blaze until it turned to smoke and embers.

Crunch. Crunch. Crunch.

Ruthie squeezed her eyes shut. Why didn't she put out the fire? After everything they'd gone through, they were almost safe, and she…she didn't put out the fire. "I'll check out the fake scree." Her voice quivered. "Do you think it's an animal?" She didn't know why she even asked.

"I don't know."

"I'm going to see." A voice deep inside Ruthie told her she didn't need to verify the threat.

"Wait, I'll get my knife and come with you."

As Ruthie walked with Moose to her creation, her stomach knotted. To think Hucklesford's presence was her fault made her burn inside with guilt.

Moose stood as still as a statue for fifteen minutes. Nothing broke the silence. He held his hand to his ear. "It's all quiet." He put his knife away.

Ruthie couldn't get the awful sound of the ice cracking out of her mind, but she said, "It appears everything's fine."

"Right, I'll start packing." Moose turned toward their campsite.

"I'll wait here to make sure we have nothing to worry about."

"Okay." Moose left.

Ruthie put her hands over her ears, hoping to destroy the racket of twigs breaking and ice cracking in her head. Tip-toeing closer to the scree, she listened for the real sound her ears didn't want to hear. Why didn't the uneasiness coursing through her go away?

Crunch. Crunch.

To keep from throwing up, she swallowed over and over. Could Hucklesford see her? Hoping to hide from him, she moved to the right side of the faux scree, where she had added rocks and Moose had heightened the barrier. She heard the sound of heavy breathing.

Chapter Twenty-Six

Nearly collapsing, Ruthie propped her body against the enormous boulder, the only thing separating her from the person sucking air in spurts. After ten minutes silence fell. A forest creature must've made the noise and now it had left. She needn't worry. No, she needn't worry at all. Everything was fine. She took a step on unsteady legs.

Someone wheezed on the other side of the scree.

Ruthie sank like a submarine on the bottom of the ocean while a destroyer crawled over it. She held onto a pole and listened to the sonar tracking. Unsteady on her feet, she forced herself to stand up, to stare at the computer, calculating the closeness of the enemy, timing the sound wave traveling to its target and returning. The destroyer was directly over her. Sailors in the control room looked like Moose and Thad. Growing weaker and weaker, Ruthie loosened her grip on the pole and dropped nearly to the submarine floor. She pulled up, staying awake to protect Moose and Thad.

Someone gasped for air on the other side of the barrier. If he attacked, would he trap her, Moose, and

Thad like the sailors or shoot them right away? She remained as motionless as the submarine lurking at the bottom of the sea. If it were Hucklesford and he crossed their fortress, she'd show him. She'd hit him with a rock. But wait. He had a rifle and probably would shoot her first—unless he didn't see her. Ruthie balled her hand into a fist and chewed her knuckle.

Huffing and puffing grew loud.

Their lives depended on what she did, and she didn't know what to do. While she understood the construction, she had no idea how to keep Hucklesford from getting through the fortress. Of course, he couldn't go through the boulder, but he could crash into the rocks. They'd roll out of his way. She rubbed her temples then crouched behind stones jutting out from the fake rockslide.

If the slope shifted, debris would tumble to the right side of it. She bit her bottom lip and scrutinized it again. Then, she hurried to tell Moose and Thad, her heart racing as she walked as fast as she could on the frozen ground.

Moose drank from his thermos.

"Someone's on the other side of our barricade."

He shot up and darted toward the entryway with Ruthie. As they walked, he whispered, "I'll stay on the right side of the wall while you hide behind the boulder. If he breaks through, he'll probably see me." He tapped his breastbone with his hand. "I'll take care of him. If something goes wrong, try to get behind him and hit him on the head before he shoots me."

Ruthie put her shaky hand to her throat and gulped. "I guess there's nowhere for us to hide."

Moose pulled together his brows. "Right."

"When we get there, keep quiet. Listen for labored breathing." Ruthie tried to speak, but her voice broke up. "Should we tell Thad?"

"Not yet."

As Ruthie and Moose approached the barrier, Moose turned toward the right side where the sound of someone wheezing filtered through the rocks.

Ruthie wanted to slap herself. What did she do wrong? Why couldn't Hucklesford accept her slope as a natural part of the cave and leave? He probably saw the fire she failed to put out reflecting off of the ice. Either way, she was to blame.

A stone fell. Then another. The faux scree rolled toward Moose. He jumped. Ruthie screamed.

Huckelsford peered at them, his eyes wild like the coyote's.

Ruthie darted to the stones beside the large boulder.

Hucklesford pointed his rifle at her.

She stood dead still, holding her breath while Moose charged through the loose stones. They tumbled, the sound rumbling in Ruthie's ears.

Moose sprang behind Hucklesford.

Grabbed him.

Hucklesford's rifle wobbled as though Thad held it. Scary, but Moose turned Hucklesford around, snatched the weapon from him, and pinned his wrists behind him. "How dare you try to harm Ruthie. I'd never let that happen." He directed his gaze to her. "Bring some of the athletic, elastic wrapping and tape."

Ruthie's throat turned bone dry. She swallowed several times. "Right away."

Hurrying to the campsite, she rummaged through

Moose's football bag, the noise waking Thad.

"What's happening?"

Ruthie sputtered, "We, we...we captured Hucklesford. Moose needs to tie him up. I'm looking for the first-aid dressings."

Thad hopped up and grabbed his rifle, which bobbed up and down more than usual in his trembling hand. "I'm going right now," he spit out the words before he left.

Ruthie threw out socks, T-shirts, and sweatpants. Finally, she snatched up the elastic wrap. Visions of Hucklesford breaking loose flashed in her brain. Slipping and skating across the frozen earth she rushed to Moose.

Thad held the rifle. It swayed up, down, right, left, and finally toward Hucklesford.

Fear danced on Hucklesford's face. "Hey, make him put down that firearm. It's liable to go off. At least the police have steady aims. They don't shoot by accident."

"I'm not a policeman. If this thing goes off, it's just an unfortunate mistake from a nervous kid."

Moose sent Thad a stiff gaze. "Put it down. I got him."

Stepping as far away from Hucklesford as she could without leaving, Ruthie leaned against the boulder in their barricade. She hoped Moose had him.

Chapter Twenty-Seven

Ruthie gazed at the scree. The only thing standing—the large boulder. The small stones lay scattered on the frozen ground. After Moose wrapped the tape around Hucklesford's wrists, she eyed the faux handcuffs. They looked flimsy.

Thad inspected them. "We should reinforce those to make sure he doesn't get loose." He balled his right hand into a fist and hit his left palm. "The way he's been trying to kill us ever since we left the house, we ought to beat him."

Ruthie gasped. "What's come over you?"

"Getting run out of my warm house and chased down makes me angry."

"Moose has him. We won't let him escape."

Thad glared at Hucklesford. "Thanks to you, we've learned to get along on three hours of sleep each night. We'll guard you day and night for as long as we have to."

Hucklesford stood before them with a poker face as blank as one of the mountain boulders. A scraggly, dirty black beard lent a wild man's touch to his appearance. Perhaps Thad reacted to Hucklesford as he should. After all, someone needed to keep him in line.

A fear of Thad probably lay behind Hucklesford's vacant stare, not because Thad appeared tough, but because he held such an unsteady grip on a deadly weapon.

Moose tightened the wrap on Hucklesford's wrist. "He's right about one thing. We won't let you out of our sight." He nodded toward Ruthie. "Look for something to strengthen these make-do shackles."

"Okay." Ruthie left.

In moments, Thad caught up to her. Thank goodness he held the rifle so it hung at his side. "I have an idea. I have wire and cutters."

"That should work."

When they reached the campsite, Thad laid down the rifle and snatched the supplies, which he handed to Ruthie before he reclaimed his weapon. "I won't get near that guy without this."

Ruthie stepped back. "Okay, but point it toward the ground and carry it carefully." She watched to make sure Thad aimed as she had asked. As long as he didn't shoot himself in the foot, they should arrive intact. They did. When Thad propped the rifle on the granite wall, she took a sigh of relief.

Moose glanced at the wire and pulled a slow grin. "Perfect." He wound the constraint over the dressing holding Hucklesford's wrists together, twisted it into a knot, and clipped it. "There."

Thad shifted his weight several times. "What are we going to do with him?"

Hucklesford smirked. "You don't even know what to do with yourself."

"We're going to turn him over to the police. Now pack up, eat a protein bar, and let's go." Moose turned toward Ruthie. "If you would, gather my things and give Thad the bags."

"I beg your pardon. I gotta' carry mine and his rifle plus my bag."

Moose shot Thad a stern look. "Give the firearms to Ruthie and take all of our bags."

Thank you, Moose.

"You kiddin' me?"

"No, we'll go straight to the two-lane road and call the police. I understand your distrust of Hucklesford, but we have a job to do and homes to visit for Christmas. We can't allow this situation to spin out of control."

Thad pulled down his eyebrows. "Okay."

"And remember to forgive him," Ruthie said.

Hucklesford spat at her, missing the side of her face by an eighth of an inch.

Moose made a fist, but stopped short of throwing a punch. "I ought to knock the daylights out of you. You do anything that even looks like that again, and I'm liable to get really angry."

Hucklesford shrank several inches.

Ruthie and Thad went for the last time to their campsite and packed everything.

When they returned to Moose and Hucklesford, Moose gave Hucklesford a shove forward. "So, Hucky boy, you seem familiar with this place. Did you grow up around here?"

"Yep."

"Did you spend lots of time playing in the woods as a kid?"

"Nope."

"Why not?" Moose pushed Hucklesford forward

again because he kept slowing down as though he searched for a way to escape.

"I worked all the time, cutting down trees, bringing in firewood, whatever my pa told me to do."

When they reached Thad's truck with the slit tires, Thad's face turned as red as the flames in their campsite fires. "Look what you did. It's a good thing I'm not carrying the rifles."

Hucklesford pasted on a sinister grin.

Ruthie's skin crawled. She couldn't comprehend the hate in him, especially his spitting when she mentioned forgiveness. His future looked sad. That bothered her. She didn't know why, but it did. "You know, Hucklesford, you've made a fine mess of your life, but it doesn't end on earth. While we're walking, give lots of thought to how you want to spend your hereafter."

"There ain't no hereafter. If one exists and I'm going to the bad place, it couldn't be worse than the here has been."

Sucking air in her nose, Ruthie created a squeak. "It can get *much* worse, but Jesus died for your salvation. To receive his gift, you only need to accept Him, confess your sins, and ask for forgiveness." Ruthie hoped he wouldn't spit on her. She hadn't meant for her words to sound pleading, but they did. She noticed a speck of softening in Hucklesford's expression.

"What day is this? You're preaching like it's Sunday," Thad said.

"Let's see. Today is Friday. I need to go home to see my parents, then return to Hilltop for football practice next week. Where's that two-lane road?"

Hucklesford guffawed, spraying spit with his evil laugh. "I think you took a wrong turn at the truck. You ain't gonna' see the local road this way."

"Oh yes, we will. Ruthie, give me that rifle."

"Nooo." Hucklesford jumped. "Don't let him touch that rifle. I'll tell you where to go. I guess I'm going to die anyway, but if I have a trial, there's a chance I'll get life."

"Out with the directions." Moose growled the words. "They better be right."

"You ain't off by much. Just make a left here and go straight. We'll get there soon. I don't guess you'd let me go if I promise not to chase you."

"You guessed right." Thad spoke loud and clear.

"Thad." Ruthie dragged out his name in disbelief. "You've got to forgive this guy for your own good. You can't know what his life's been like because you haven't lived it. Only God can judge him. Not you. Jesus knows Hucklesford's pain and sorrow. If he'll confess his sins and accept Jesus..."

"Will you shut up with the Jesus stuff?"

Ruthie flinched. The rage in Hucklesford's remark pierced her heart. If anyone ever needed to hear about Jesus, he did.

Thad cracked his knuckles.

"If you want to know the truth, I ain't never killed nobody."

"What?" Moose's mouth gaped.

Thad stumbled. "You're kidding."

Ruthie's breath hitched. "No?'

"Yes, and I'm probably going to die for something I didn't do."

Chapter Twenty-Eight

Ruthie pondered Hucklesford's situation as she walked toward the truck stop. Was he serious about not killing anyone? More than likely, he would face a death sentence. "The news said you murdered three people." Confusion pounded in her brain like a drum. "If you didn't do it, you need to hire a good lawyer and prove it. Your future looks pretty dim right now. Why aren't you at the police station declaring your innocence?"

Hucklesford blinked. "I came here, so I could live the rest of my days in peace."

"You expect peace? Do you think law enforcement will overlook what you've done?" The irritation inside Ruthie rushed out with every word.

Hucklesford grimaced. "I didn't know you'd butt in."

Ruthie gasped.

"If you didn't murder those people, why were you trying to kill us?" Thad asked.

"Ha. I could've killed all of you a bunch of times." He pointed his finger at Thad. "I've had plenty of chances to shoot you since you been living in that fancy house."

Thad stood with his feet a foot and a half apart. "Why didn't you?"

Hucklesford took a stride toward Thad. "I told you. I ain't no murderer."

"Whew." Moose swiped his forehead. "Let's sit down for a minute. I want to hear what Hucklesford has to say."

Moose sat on a boulder and patted it. Hucklesford joined him, his eyebrows pulled into a V over his nose. Thad and Ruthie brushed the snow off of two tree stumps across from them and sat down.

Ruthie couldn't imagine what Hucklesford would tell them. After fulfilling a teaching assistantship and then instructing youngsters, she usually could judge whether a student told the truth by paying close attention to the person's body language. She'd never tried it with a murderer, but she would now—for Hucklesford's sake.

Moose turned toward Hucklesford. "We're all ears."

"Okay, I robbed those jewelry stores. There were three of us. We wore masks, so it was hard to tell who was who." He shifted his weight. "I didn't even have a gun, but Joey, one of the other guys, did. He stood two inches away from me on my right and fired with his left hand. I guess it looked like I did it." He stuck out his lower lip like a child about to cry. "I couldn't believe he wiped out those people. When I agreed to help with the robbery, they told me no one would get hurt, let alone killed."

Ruthie noted how Hucklesford made eye contact with Moose and blinked very little. He spoke with a steady voice without sputtering. Judging from what she observed, especially his mouth, which now looked like he was about to throw up, he told the truth.

Thad glared at Hucklesford. "So, it's okay with you to take other people's stuff as long as you don't have to kill them."

"My mother would hide in shame and disappointment because of who I am. She tried to raise me right, but my pa was so mean. Mom tried to make up for it by telling me I could work hard and make something of my life." Hucklesford glanced down. "She must've known I had little chance of that, but wanted to give me hope." He looked up with eyes swimming in sorrow. "Life ain't worth living when someone takes away all your hope. After she died, that's what happened to me. I had no hope, no way to better myself, and no reason to try, but being poor got old. When I met Joey and Stevie in a pool hall in Misty Ridge, they were the first good friends I'd ever had. And they had money, lots of it." Hucklesford's voice rose in excitement when he said lots of it.

Ruthie focused on Hucklesford. Would he give her a reason to change her opinion about him telling the truth when he said he didn't kill anyone?

"I ain't never had any money and ain't got no way to make any." He scuffed up ice with his boot. "I didn't murder nobody. If I only thought about hurting someone, it would've killed my mother if she hadn't died already. I just never would."

When he spoke about his mother, he peered into the distance as though his words took him to a place far away from his current situation.

Ruthie believed him.

"Ha." Thad let out a laugh full of razor blades.

"Answer me. Why were you shooting at us? Why did you slit the tires on my truck?"

"I don't know. After everything that's gone on, I ain't thinking straight. I figured if I scared you, you'd be too afraid to tell anybody where I was. Or maybe I hoped you wouldn't tell. Like I said, I don't know. I don't know anything anymore. I'm just trying to survive."

Moose removed his toboggan and ran his hand through his hair. "Oh boy, what are we going to do with you?"

Hucklesford's face opened as wide as a dinner plate. "Let me go. I won't hurt nobody, and there's nothing to steal up here."

Ruthie looked at Thad.

"I don't want nothing outta' his fancy house." Hucklesford rubbed his beard against his shoulder.

Ruthie sized up the gesture and decided he wasn't straying from the truth, but instead, the scraggly beard with long, uneven strands of hair stuck together with oil and dirt, itched.

Moose let out a loud sigh. "I believe you. You could've shot us when we left the cabin. There were other occasions when it appeared you simply missed us. You're claiming you failed to hit us on purpose?"

"Right. I didn't aim at you. I fired left of you." He shifted his weight. "I hit the ice beside your boot. I got closer than I thought I would."

Thad snorted. "Sure you did."

"I'm no marksman. I never had fired a gun until I hooked up with Stevie and Joey."

Moose nodded. "You're going to need a lot of help. Let's do this. When we turn you over to the police, if you promise you won't try to escape, we'll tell them about this discussion. As far as I'm concerned, if you do everything we ask, it's the same as turning yourself in." He directed his gaze to Ruthie and Thad. "How about you guys?"

Ruthie gave Moose a thumbs up.

Thad cocked an eyebrow and kept silent for what seemed like ten minutes.

Moose sent him a stern look. "We don't have forever."

Thad smirked. "If you say so."

Hucklesford scowled. "Why would I do that?"

"It will give you validity. We'll ask them to examine the tape closer to see if they can tell Joey's firing instead of you."

"Wouldn't you know it would blur? Ain't that just a fine bucket of worms? I couldn't get a break if my life depended on it. Come to think of it, it does."

Thad got up and leaned over Hucklesford like a schoolteacher in a student's face, trying to make a point. "Man, it's no wonder you're in such a mess. That's exactly what Moose is doing. He's trying to give you a break. You're not cooperating. If you know what's good for you, you'll listen to him and stop moaning and groaning about what you don't have. Lots of us don't have everything we want." Thad sat down on the tree stump and folded his hands in his lap.

Hucklesford snarled at Thad, then directed his attention to Moose. "All right, tell me what you want me to do."

"First, apologize to Ruthie."

Hucklesford glared at Ruthie. Finally, he said, "I'm sorry I spat at ye. I don't see where having faith has ever done me much good, so I stopped having it, but I shouldn't have taken that out on you. Least that's what my mama would say."

Hucklesford needed to hear a sermon, but this wasn't the time or place. "I accept your apology."

Hucklesford turned toward Moose. "What else?"

Chapter Twenty-Nine

Moose ran a stick around the ground then he let his eyes meet Hucklesford's. "You need a shave to look presentable. Before I call the police in Misty Ridge, we'll find a men's room where we can handle that." Moose rubbed the side of his face. "I have a friend at the college who's a lawyer. I'll talk to him about your defense."

"I can't pay no lawyer."

"I'll work something out with him to do it pro bono."

"What's that?"

"Pro bono means you don't have to pay."

"Oh." Hucklesford got a blank expression. "I'm still going to prison because I robbed the jewelry store."

"That's probably true, but my friend might arrange a lesser sentence if you're willing to give the authorities information on Joey and Stevie, especially Joey."

Hucklesford shrugged. "I should've been a lawyer. This is interesting stuff."

Thad stood and stretched. "You should've been anything but a criminal."

"With God, all things are possible. I'm adding one

more requirement to Moose's list. I'll bring you a Bible, and you will read it." Ruthie sent Hucklesford her most authoritative teacher stare. "If you are well-behaved and show promise in prison, they might send you to school to learn a trade."

"I woulda' made a good detective." He peered into the distance.

"Yeah, you know what the thugs are doing," Thad said.

Moose stood and pulled Hucklesford up with him.

Ruthie got up too. Then they walked down a slick hill toward the surface road. She held onto tree boughs, but Thad didn't until he slipped. Afterward, he followed Ruthie limb for limb.

Moose grabbed tree branches with one hand and held on to Hucklesford with the other while Hucklesford rotated his body right, then left. Was he trying to pull down Moose and get away? Ruthie tipped him a poison gaze. He didn't stand a chance against Moose with Moose's muscular build and broad shoulders. Hucklesford must've finally realized that because he quit wiggling.

Could someone as defiant as Hucklesford ever change? It was worth a try. An opportunity to help someone faced Thad, Moose, and her. Could they give him some of the hope that vanished when his mother died? They'd have to do it even though the law had labeled him a fleeing felon.

Ruthie studied him. Instead of an angry criminal, she saw a pitiful human being. Yet, she was a college advanced grammar professor, not a policewoman or a social worker. Her head ached. Once they turned him over to the police, they'd done their job, but she meant what she said about giving him a Bible to keep him company in prison.

After hearing his story, she would not only squeeze all the fun she could out of every second after escaping this forest with her life, she would do all she could to help those less fortunate before it was too late for them. She yearned to see Hucklesford and others like him turn to God and have a better life. After finishing grad school because of her parents' desire for her to have a better salary than they did, then staying pent up to learn about nouns and verbs, she now realized there was so much more to live for than money and English grammar.

She spotted an object in the distance. A road sign? She squinted, then bounced on her toes and clapped. "Look. Look. There's the two-lane road."

Hucklesford jerked forward. Moose held him steady.

"I was happy here. I ain't going to bother nobody. Please, let me go."

Ruthie's heart cried to give in and let him flee to contentment, but it wasn't the right thing to do. She looked at Moose. He wanted to let him go too. She could see it in his pinched face, but Moose would turn him over to the police.

Finally, they set foot on the ice and snow covering the surface road. Ruthie pulled her cell phone from her purse and squealed. "I have a signal." She held her phone high.

Thad reached in his pants pocket and pulled out his. His face lit up like a Christmas tree. "I do too! I'm calling Dad right now." He stepped away from Moose, Ruthie, and Hucklesford and chatted on his cell for a few minutes.

After he returned, Moose asked, "Do you know which way to go to find the gas station?"

"Yeah, ah, Hodge's Truck Stop about a mile from here."

Moose's features grew tight. "These rifles won't fit in any of our bags." He cast his gaze to his football gear, then picked it up. "I'll put them in here as far as they'll go, then zip it around the stocks." He glanced at Thad. "Hold him for a second."

Thad grasped Hucklesford's arm. "It's a pleasure."

Hucklesford made a snorting, guttural sound as he gave Thad a dirty look.

Moose removed the bullets from Thad and Hucklesford's riffles and placed them in the bag. "When we get to the truck stop, we'll do something with that beard."

Thad shifted his weight from one side to the other. "We who?"

"You and me, of course. Ruthie can't go in the men's room."

"You want me to help shave him?"

Hucklesford recoiled. "Nooooo."

"Just cut it," Moose said.

Within thirty minutes, they reached the truck stop, a red and white one-story, 20,000-square-foot, warehouse-type building on four-and-a-half acres. Drivers filled their cars with gas and meandered back and forth between the parking lot and the front door. Transfer trucks sat in a huge paved area behind the structure.

At the glass entryway, Moose spread his legs wide and stood in front of Hucklesford. "I'm going to un-cuff you to keep the manager from suspecting you're a criminal and calling the police. Walk beside me and don't make a move toward escaping. Ruthie will stay ready to punch 911 on her cell while Thad buys the scissors and a razor. If Ruthie makes the emergency call, you lose our support when you tell your side of the robbery. Do you understand?"

Hucklesford inhaled, blew air through his nose, then mumbled a faint "yes."

Apparently, Moose accepted the gesture because he unwound the wire and bandages before the four of them walked inside the truck stop. People checking out the groceries, video games, and souvenirs filled the building.

Ruthie glimpsed her first Christmas decoration—a tree with blinking red, green, and white lights sitting in a corner near the entrance. Overhead, silver tinsel draped across the ceiling added glitter. "Ah," she let out a tiny gasp.

She questioned whether Moose made the right decision when he untied Hucklesford to give him a break, but what really bothered her…Just in case Moose's judgement proved wrong, he held her responsible for seeing a problem and pressing 911. She scrutinized Hucklesford's every move, trying to discern what he might do next.

After several minutes, he moved his arm upward. Ruthie shoved her shaking finger on 9, but he picked up a can from the shelf in front of him and read something on it. Within two minutes, he put it down and walked to his right.

Moose flinched like a race horse ready to charge out of its stall.

Hucklesford stopped at a display of American flags. He tilted his head and eyed them from each side as though he didn't understand what they were. Did he comprehend the symbol of freedom and opportunity applied to his life, even now?

It seemed like another century passed, but finally Thad brought Moose the items. Moose purchased them from a tall, skinny kid with blond hair, who looked to be around eighteen.

The kid gave Moose his change and directed his gaze toward Hucklesford. "I guess he's the one you're buying the scissors and razor for. He needs to do something with that beard."

Hucklesford snarled, his moustache wiggling like a fuzzy worm.

"Yeah, he's had a bit of a rough spell, but we're going to fix him up," Moose said.

Thad's eyelashes blinked like windshield wipers turned on high. "He's had a rough spell? He's had a rough spell, my eye. He's..."

Wrinkles cut across Moose's forehead. "Shhh."

Ruthie agreed. Moose needed to quiet Thad. So far, so good with Hucklesford. He'd acted exactly as Moose told him to. There was no reason to antagonize him and change that.

The three men entered the restroom.

Trying to block the image of Hucklesford attacking Moose and Thad, Ruthie paced between a sign that read *Showers This Way* and the video games. Moose would keep Hucklesford under control—she hoped.

Chapter Thirty

In the restroom, Moose pointed to a gray laminate vanity with three sinks. "Wash that beard with soap from the dispenser."

Hucklesford stared at Moose with eyes of stone. He bent over and did as Moose said though. Then he stood and looked at Moose like one of Moose's football players getting a lecture he didn't want.

Moose turned toward Thad. "I'll watch him while you trim that beard as close to his face as you can without nicking him."

Thad stumbled around. "You're kidding, aren't you?"

"No, I'm serious. Just cut it. I'll make sure he doesn't move."

"Okay. Here goes." Thad let out a quick, disgusted snort. "Don't you even think about moving."

"Don't worry. I'm afraid you might handle scissors like you do a rifle." Hucklesford growled.

Thad knitted his eyebrows. "I resent that, and I'm the one holding the scissors."

"Okay, get on with it," Moose said.

Thad grasped a wad of the beard and snipped. Then he repeated the action, holding out handfuls of it, cutting them until finally Hucklesford sported short whiskers. Thad stepped away from him. "I'm done."

"All right, I'll finish and you watch. I don't think he'll try anything with a razor close to his throat."

Hucklesford shivered. "I don't never want to see a piece of jewelry again as long as I live."

Moose shaved the sideburns. "You're about to begin a long, hard journey, but you're young. Cooperate with the police and become a model prisoner. It's up to you to earn a second chance at life, maybe become a private detective too. I know one, Nick Lancaster. He could use you as a sidekick as long as he could trust you."

As Moose rinsed the razor, he shot Thad a stern stare to let him know he should not discourage Hucklesford.

Thad ran his finger in front of his lips as if he zipped them shut.

Moose continued shaving. "Working for Nick would take a lot of hard work and good, clean living. As Ruthie said, all things are possible with God. Remember that." Moose swiped the razor the last time then eyed his job. "All right, wash your face and let's get this over with. There are Christian people who will help you if you turn your life over to God."

"God? There ain't no…God don't want nothing to do with the likes of me."

"Yes, He does. He loves you more than your mother did. He wants you to have a good life. I bet your mother told you that."

Hucklesford lowered his eyelids, then he turned

toward the sink, splashed water on his face and dried it with a paper towel, wiping the corners of his eyes when he finished.

Thad gazed at Hucklesford. "All shined up, he looks like a clean-cut guy. I guess I could see him as a PI, but that's going to take a lot of effort and probably help from some influential people."

Moose gave Thad a narrow-eyed expression. He imagined underneath Hucklesford's hard exterior he hurt so badly he believed he could never overcome his pain and shortcomings. Unfortunately, everyone didn't get to start their lives in the same place. Hucklesford began his with little chance of success and happiness. Moose hoped the police would research his story and find he didn't have a gun. He intended to pray for Hucklesford, and what about Ruthie? So like the Christian teacher in her to give Hucklesford a Bible.

Moose meant to give Hucklesford a firm command, but when he said, "All right, we're ready," he couldn't keep the sadness out of his voice because a young man who already had a terrible start to his existence worsened it. If only Hucklesford could know the love of Jesus and turn things around.

They came out of the men's room and Ruthie, who waited beside the door, blinked. "Wow! You look nice."

The longer Moose waited to turn over Hucklesford, the more the coach in him wished he could help him instead. Unfortunately, Hucklesford wasn't one of his players who needed a little guidance. He motioned to Ruthie. "Call 911. Tell them to meet us outdoors on the right side of the building. There's no need to create a scene out front."

~

Ruthie made the call, then they walked outdoors and waited. Finally, the temperature warmed up, the sun melting icicles hanging from the roof of the building. Tiny puddles formed on the cement and blurred as tears of joy for her and sadness for Hucklesford filled Ruthie's eyes.

She phoned her mom and dad. When she heard their voices, it was all she could do to keep from squealing and yelling. After she clicked off the call, she held out the phone. "My mom and dad," she said to Thad, Moose, and Hucklesford.

Thad and Moose nodded. Then they all stood silent until a police car roared to them and stopped. When a stocky officer in a blue uniform hopped out with a scowl on his face, Ruthie's hope for Hucklesford telling his side of the robbery diminished. Moose was a man of his word though.

"Hi officer, I'm Ruthie O'Donnell." She pointed to Moose. "This is Coach George Byer." She motioned toward Thad. "Thad Smith." She waved her hand toward Hucklesford. "The suspect, Damian Hucklesford."

"I'm Officer Praeger. I'll take him, then get your statements." The officer charged toward Hucklesford.

Did he assume they couldn't wait to get rid of him? If so, as far as Ruthie was concerned, he'd be right. Even though she ached inside for Hucklesford's life and situation, she wanted to be free of him. Knowing Moose, he wouldn't turn Hucklesford over until Officer Praeger met Moose's conditions.

Sure enough, Moose placed his arm in front of Hucklesford. "No."

Officer Praeger glared at Moose. "What do you mean, no?"

"He turned himself in and told us he didn't commit the murders in the recent jewelry store robbery. I gave him my word you would let him explain what happened." Moose clenched his jaw. "I coach young men about his age. When I give my word, especially to a young man, it's good. I'm not turning him over until you hear him out."

Tension thicker than the air on a foggy night in these mountains hung in the air.

"What do you think you're going to do with him with me standing right here?"

Moose locked intense eyes with Officer Praeger.

Ruthie stood ready to run.

Finally, Officer Praeger said, "All right." Then he addressed Hucklesford. "You have the right to remain silent. Anything you say can and will be used against you in a court of law. You have the right to an attorney. If you cannot afford an attorney, one will be appointed for you." He cuffed Hucklesford. "Let's hear it."

"Tell him what you told us." Moose's tone sounded like he encouraged a five-year-old.

Ruthie found it odd Hucklesford had the gumption to commit robbery, but appeared too weak to defend himself. If she had to guess, and that's all she could do, she supposed Stevie and Joey filled a need buried deep in Hucklesford's soul. They convinced him they were his friends.

"All right." Hucklesford spoke in a soft, quivering voice. "I took part in the robbery, but I didn't shoot nobody. I didn't even fire a gun. Joey stood to my side. He's the one who killed those people." Hucklesford gagged. "I was afraid I'd throw up in the store. It makes me sick to talk about it."

Officer Praeger stepped a foot farther away from Hucklesford.

Ruthie fidgeted with her sleeve, hoping this conversation ended before Hucklesford upchucked.

"As I mentioned, I heard on the news the tape blurred. Still, the store clerk identified me as the..." Hucklesford gulped and made a choking noise.

Ruthie stiffened.

"He made me as the killer. Joey's left-handed. He shot from my right side, making it look like I did it." Hucklesford's chin trembled. "I wonder if they planned that from the beginning." He swallowed hard, his throat lurching before he cleared it.

Even after all he'd been through his entire life, he faced something much worse than his childhood. He clearly understood that, or he wouldn't have worked so hard to avoid it. At least he found the fortitude to tell Officer Praeger his side of the robbery without throwing up.

Officer Praeger let out a puff of air and looked at Moose. "I never. Do you believe him?"

"Yes. He did the right thing. He turned himself in."

"We haven't caught the other two." Officer Praeger mumbled the words to himself. Then he directed his gaze to Husklesford. "If you could give us information leading to their arrest, your attorney might plead for leniency for your part in the robbery."

Hucklesford smirked.

Moose's eyebrows shot up. "We'll make sure he shares what he knows." He directed a hard stare at Hucklesford.

Officer Praeger's eyes widened. "Any offer, if one's made, will be contingent on whether we can prove you're telling the truth."

"Of course, I'm telling the truth." Hucklesford's firm reply resounded so loud a bird sitting on a nearby tree limb flew away.

Officer Praeger turned to Thad.

Hucklesford never moved or changed his expression. Fear glinted in his eyes when he cast them toward Thad, though.

Moose gave Thad a pleading look.

"I'm here because I met Ruthie and Moose, uh Dr. O'Donnell and Coach Byer, at a house my father owns. I let them spend the night to get out of the cold."

Ruthie took a sigh of relief.

The officer turned toward Moose. "But you knew Hucklesford was close by?"

Grateful to stand in safety in a parking lot, Ruthie ran one of the football shoes Moose had loaned her in a circle on the pavement. Swishing the water from the ice melting off of the building, she gazed at the ripples while she waited for Moose's reply.

"Ruthie had heard a news announcement stating he'd fled to the North Carolina Mountains. The bulletin reported the police searched the Appalachian Trail and found no sign of him, so we figured he was in this area."

Ruthie looked up. "Right. Moose and I wrecked our cars at the dangerous curve on the interstate just outside of Hilltop College. The hood of my vehicle went through the guardrail and hit a tree, and Moose, uh, Coach Byer, slid into the guardrail. Moose told me about a cabin where we could find shelter. Once we reached the old house and went inside, we noticed it appeared occupied. Fearing the murderer on the loose might live in it, we left."

Officer Praeger glanced at Hucklesford, who nodded.

Then the officer knitted his brows and glanced at his notes. "Dr. O'Donnell, could you explain how you ended up roaming around in the woods and went to Thad's home?" Urgency lined his voice. "I'm trying to put the pieces together, but something's missing."

Ruthie didn't know what to say. As she glimpsed Moose, to her surprise, Hucklesford stepped forward.

"I was frightened."

"You were frightened? Ha!" Ruthie gave Hucklesford her evil eye.

"I was. I ain't killed no one. Like I told you, I figured hiding in the hills was the best way to live the rest of my life in peace. I followed you and Moose to scare you away. I told myself if I could hide out long enough, in time everyone would just forget about it."

Officer Praeger's face turned flaming red. "We don't forget murder." He shifted his weight. "But to the matter before us, Dr. O'Donnell and Coach Byer left the cabin, and you followed them."

'Yes."

"Then what did you do?"

"I fired a rifle, but like I said, I ain't no murderer. I never intended to hit them, never even nicked them."

All he put them through was a game to scare them? Ruthie balled her hand into a fist.

Hucklesford pulled back his shoulders. "I saved their lives." He pointed to Moose and Ruthie.

Ruthie placed her hand on her chest. "Huh?"

Moose's eyes snapped wide.

"You what?" Officer Praeger asked.

"That's right. There was a catamount about to pounce on them before I shot it. I told you I ain't no murderer. I just wanted to scare them away, so they'd leave me alone."

"You…" Ruthie couldn't get out the words. "You shot it instead of us."

"Yep."

Ruthie stamped her foot. "I don't believe you."

Officer Praeger glanced at Moose, then Ruthie and Thad. "Even if he spared two lives, he's accused of killing three people. We can't sort this out today. Even if we could, he needs a trial." He pulled a notepad from his pocket and handed it to Moose. "Write down your names, addresses, and phone numbers. Then you can go and I'll take Hucklesford."

"Where?" Moose asked before he set pen to paper.

"To the jail in Misty Ridge to start. Then we'll go from there."

Ruthie and Thad added their information and gave it to Officer Praeger.

"We need more citizens like you three. Call if you think of anything else." Officer Praeger gave each of them a card.

Moose held up his. "Will do. I'm going to arrange for a friend of mine to represent Hucklesford."

"Okay." Officer Praeger left with Hucklesford.

Ruthie watched Hucklesford get in the police car, then turned toward Moose. "What do you think will happen to him?"

"I don't know."

Chapter Thirty-One

The sun cut through the fog creating a wide ray of light on the truck stop entrance. Hope rose inside Ruthie for her new life. Would Hucklesford get a second chance too?

Thad rose on his tiptoes. "My dad had landed at Misty Ridge Airport and rented an SUV. He's coming to get me. I'm sure he will take you and Moose to get your cars. Let's eat at one of the sandwich shops inside while we wait."

"Sounds good to me," Ruthie said.

Moose, Ruthie, and Thad strolled into the truck stop and entered a deli with booths with red plastic seats and a large window overlooking the parking lot. After they ordered, Ruthie savored every bite of her turkey sandwich. She wasn't sure which she relished more, the sandwich, or the heat warming her muscles aching from staying ready to run in freezing temperatures for so long. She stared at the tiny Christmas tree on their table, a Christmas carol wafted into the dining area. She was almost home.

Thad jumped up. "Dad."

Dressed in a navy suit and tie, a tall, thin man with

sun-kissed skin ran to Thad and grabbed him in a bear hug. After he let go, he rubbed Thad's arm. "Son, I'm so glad you're alright." He held Thad out. "Let me see. You look fine. Yes, you do. Just fine."

"I'm okay, Dad." Thad turned toward Ruthie and Moose. "These are my friends, Dr. Ruthie O'Donnell and Coach George Byer."

"Hi, Thaddeus Smith." He extended his hand, and Moose and Ruthie shook it.

"Sit down, Dad. Do you want lunch?"

Thad scooted in the seat across from Ruthie and Moose, and Mr. Smith went to the counter. He returned with a grilled cheese sandwich and a glass of tea. "Thad tells me the two of you helped him escape a killer. I'm so grateful. How can I repay you?"

Ruthie and Moose opened their mouths. Moose motioned for Ruthie to go first.

"There's nothing to repay. After we wrecked our cars during the storm and wandered through the forest in freezing temperatures, Thad let us spend the night in your house. Honestly, I'm not sure I could have survived another twenty-four hours in this weather."

Concern washed over Mr. Smith's face. "I'm sorry."

"We're fine. Moose kept us alive as we went from campsite to campsite trying to find help, or civilization. It's Moose and I who are indebted to Thad."

"Good. I'm glad my son could help." Mr. Smith's eyes softened. "I'm going to take him home. He's never coming here again in the winter. I counted on nature, the tranquility of the mountains, and getting away from the noise of the city to allow him to think about his future. I was so wrong. Maybe, in the spring."

Thad arched his eyebrows. "I thought about it."

Mr. Smith shifted in his seat. "Good, son. That's good. Let's try to get you into UNC Spring Semester."

Thad sent a look to Moose.

Moose lowered his chin in a nod.

"Moose, uh Coach Byer, needs a student trainer to help with Hilltop College's bowl game and take care of end-of-the-season duties."

"Uh, well, I hope he'll find one."

"Dad, you don't understand."

"What don't I understand?"

"I could enroll in their business school and work with Coach Byer for at least one year. Then if you still preferred, I go to UNC, but..." Thad took a deep breath. "I might want a career as an athletic trainer instead of an executive."

"What?" Mr. Smith slumped. "Now Son..."

Ruthie bit her tongue to keep from advising Mr. Smith he should listen to Thad.

Thad cowered. "I came to these hills to get my priorities straight because you told me I had to." Defeat lined his voice.

Moose squirmed while Ruthie twisted the button on her jacket.

"You might think you know what you want, but you don't understand what it's like to pull yourself up by your bootstraps and make something of your life. It isn't easy. You need an excellent education, a useful major, and a good job." The type of authority very few questioned rang in Mr. Smith's voice.

"No, I don't know about pulling myself up by my boots, or tennis shoes, or any other footwear, but I want to enroll in classes at Hilltop College." Thad pleaded.

The expression on Thad's face would've made Ruthie say yes. She couldn't help but stare at Mr. Smith.

"It's not the caliber of education I want for you." Mr. Smith shifted his gaze to Moose. "No slight intended."

Moose ran his finger around his coffee cup for several seconds. "None taken."

Ruthie figured he said it for Thad's sake.

"I've only worked at Hilltop one semester, but I can say my students will leave my class with superior grammar skills."

Moose snickered. "She's not kidding. She's a walking advanced grammar book."

Mr. Smith eyed Ruthie, then zeroed in on Thad.

Apparently, Mr. Smith had worked hard to get where he was. It seemed he intended to pass that success to Thad. Ruthie understood all too well, but it appeared God gave Mr. Smith and Thad different talents and desires. At least, she had characteristics of her mom and dad and enjoyed her students. Fortunately, no other profession had called to her as it had to Moose and Thad. If only Mr. Smith could see that.

Ruthie peered at Mr. Smith's long fingers working around his collar, pulling on it, then unbuttoning the first button on his shirt as though it squeezed his throat. With his face twisted, Mr. Smith looked at Thad.

Ruthie feared the worst.

"Hilltop College has a fine reputation. If that's what you really want, we'll see about getting you enrolled for spring semester. You can stay for one year and we'll go from there."

Thad sprang up, nearly coming off of his seat. "Uh,

really. That's great." He flashed all of his teeth. "I can't believe it. Thank you, Dad."

Mr. Smith turned toward Moose. "How will he work for you if he isn't already a student?"

Ruthie wasn't sure if Mr. Smith sounded more resigned or disappointed, but she supposed a little of both. Hopefully, after Thad had been at Hilltop a while, Mr. Smith would think better of the school and Thad's decision.

"Student employees show up before the semester starts."

"I see. When will he need to report?" Sadness lined his tone.

Ruthie sensed Mr. Smith wanted Thad to visit with the family more than a few days. Odd. He'd sent him to the mountains. Did he miss him all of a sudden, or did he realize he was fortunate Thad survived the storm and Hucklesford? It wasn't any of her business. She'd take most of her two weeks and head back to the college on December 30th."

"The bowl game is December twenty-third. After I spend a couple of days at home, I'm returning to the school and join my assistant, who's started practice. If you'd like Thad to stay home for a week or so, he could return by the twenty-first. We'll put him to work right away then."

"Dad, pleeease."

Mr. Smith placed his palms on the table. "All right, if we're going to do this, we'll do it right. We'll find him a place to stay, even if it's only temporary."

Moose snapped his fingers. "The young man who graduated vacated an apartment." He pulled a piece of paper from his pants' pocket, wrote on it, and gave it to

Mr. Smith. "Here's the address and phone number. I've given Thad the information I'll need to give to the school to arrange for his enrollment, so he can start work."

Thad sat as proud as a peacock as he shifted his gaze between Moose and his father.

Mr. Smith nodded. "I'll have his grades..." he gathered his brows as though it pained him to say grades... "ah, hem, transferred. I suppose he'll come home after the game and stay until after Christmas."

"Yes. I'll ask for a rush on his admittance. Unless there's a snafu, he should start classes in January."

Mr. Smith put the paper in his wallet. "Let's go, son. We have lots to do."

"Can we take Ruthie and Moose to the impound lot to pick up their cars?"

Mr. Smith cut his gaze to Moose. "Of course."

"Thank you," Moose said.

After they left tips on the table, they went outside and settled into Mr. Smith's rental SUV. After he took the wheel, he asked, "Does anyone know the impound lot address?"

"Yes, it's 202 Broken Arrow Parkway in Misty Ridge," Moose answered.

Mr. Smith fiddled with something on the dashboard. "Ahh, I have it."

Within an hour, Ruthie and Moose picked up their vehicles.

Before Ruthie left the impound lot, she thanked Mr. Smith, shook hands with him, and hugged Thad and Moose. Once inside her car, she rubbed her hands around the steering wheel. Finally, she was on the way to Florida. The detour she'd taken on her way home for

Christmas had changed her life forever.

~

After enjoying the Winter Break, including a celebration of Jesus' birth with Mom, Dad, an aunt, uncle, and three cousins, Ruthie left for Hilltop College on December 30th, as planned. She reached the mountainous area on a crisp, clear day, so different from the day she left. When she parked in her driveway, the small white-frame house nestled in the valley shined in the sun and in her heart.

After she unpacked her clothes, she plopped down on the leather sofa in the living room, picked up her cell phone, and punched in a number. "It's Ruthie O'Donnell letting you know I will attend the departmental New Year's social." She clicked off, answered her next invitation, and repeated the action until finally she reached the last one. "Hi Moose, I'm home. I'm looking forward to learning about first downs, pass interference, and holding penalties along with punts, kick-offs and extra points."

Moose chuckled. "We'll watch lots of games. By the time they play the Super Bowl, you'll be an expert."

~

By February, when she and Moose held a Super Bowl party at his house, Ruthie understood the game. She and Moose invited their colleagues and Hilltop football players. The game pitted a California team against one in North Carolina, making the event even more special.

Wearing a pair of black pants and a gold shirt, representing her team's colors, the one from North Carolina, of course, Ruthie worked in Moose's recently remodeled kitchen sporting brand new granite counters and stainless-steel appliances. Moose, also dressed in gold and black, snuck up behind her and gave her a big hug. "Thank you for preparing all the extras to go with the ham and turkey. The game's about to start."

"You're welcome. I'll take out the hors de 'oeuvres, or horse doovers, as you call them."

Moose chuckled as Thad, dressed in black pants and a gold shirt, appeared in the kitchen. "I see you're ready to serve the horse doovers." He scooped up a couple of trays. "I'll pass them out."

Ruthie smiled at him. "That's nice of you, but I can set them on the coffee table."

"I want to talk to everyone," Thad said as he stepped from the kitchen to the great room. In moments, Ruthie and Moose joined twenty-five fans staring at a large wall-mounted television while Thad meandered among them with the hors d'oeuvres until they were all gone. Even though the room was nice-sized with a sofa and several easy chairs, Moose had brought in straight-backed and folding chairs for extra seating. He, Ruthie, and Thad sat in one of those.

At kickoff, the North Carolina team received the ball. Within seven plays, they took it in for a touchdown. Ruthie jumped up, clapped, and hollered.

Professor Starr, one of Ruthie's guests from the English department, turned in his seat, and gazed at her over his half-lens glasses. "You've become quite the fan, Ruthie, more so than any advanced grammar professor I've ever known."

"They don't know what they're missing." Ruthie leaned toward the television. "That's not pass interference. Boo."

Professor Starr jumped up. "Yeah, you need to get

glasses, ref."

Moose leaned back and guffawed.

Fortunately, for Ruthie, Moose, and Professor Starr, the North Carolina team won. Not long afterward, the guests left.

Ruthie loved experiencing this high point in Moose's world. She picked up paper plates, napkins, and glasses and went to the kitchen. The preparation had tired her, but the excitement of entertaining her and Moose's friends to watch the game of the season still hovered over her like morning mist in the mountains.

As she put the serving platters in the dishwasher, she recalled a time when she helped coordinate a dance at the college where she worked when she earned her PhD. A cute girl asked a shy guy to dance. He grasped her hand and swayed to the beat in seconds. "I'm coming out of my shell," he had said.

She nodded. Just like her, except she had to roam around a frozen forest to realize she was in a shell.

Moose mopped the floor then pivoted and whistled as he wiped off the kitchen counter. Then he faced Ruthie and grinned. "I'll have Thad working hard in the equipment room tomorrow. He wore himself out carrying around trays of finger food and drinks tonight. I hope it wasn't too much."

Ruthie smiled. She was proud of Thad. "He's young. He'll be fine. I'm glad his father let him attend Hilltop."

"Me too. Thank you for this get together. I couldn't have done it without you. And to think, if we hadn't met on that terrible night when we nearly went over a cliff, we probably wouldn't know each other." Moose drew her close, holding her tight as though he never wanted to let go. He gave her a long, passionate kiss. After he released her, he said, "I'll take you home. Not that I want to, but we have classes to teach in the morning."

Moose walked her to his SUV and let her in. Then he scooted into the driver's seat and started down the mountain to the valley.

Ruthie pondered Moose's remarks about them meeting in an ice storm. "I've written Hucklesford and sent him a devotional. I received a letter from him last week. It sounded as though he's changing." An ache formed in her heart. "Even if I talked to him, I wouldn't know if he were sincere or not, if his past would always haunt him, or if he could overcome it. If only he would turn to God."

Moose drummed his thumb on the steering wheel. "I've been to see him three times. Believe it or not, Thad's written to him a few times."

"No."

"Yeah, it's true."

"Deep down Thad probably understands Hucklesford started his life in a hole, and we're all he has. You probably had a lot to do with his perception of Hucklesford and the world in general. You're a wonderful influence."

Moose glanced at Ruthie; his eyes wide. "Why, thank you. I try."

He pulled up in the drive, parked, and let Ruthie out of the car. As they walked to her door, he said, "We should think of encouraging Hucklesford as an opportunity and a responsibility. Our paths crossed for a reason."

"I agree. We'll support him when he gets out. I

don't know when that will happen, or what we'll do, but we'll work it out. If he tries to get his life together and become a Christian right in our faces, what kind of Christians would we be if we didn't help him?"

"He probably saved our lives when he shot the catamount above us. We'll never know whether or not the big cat was hungry." Moose gave Ruthie a quick peck on her cheek before she went inside.

For now, she would write Hucklesford, remind him to read the Bible she gave him, and say prayers for him. Even if he got out on parole, she didn't have any idea how to help a released criminal. She yawned. She was so tired. That was a conundrum for another day.

Chapter Thirty-Two

Two and one-half years later, Ruthie, Thad, and Moose stood on the free side of the fence in front of the high walls around the prison at Misty Ridge and waited for Hucklesford.

He came out waving and grinning as though he couldn't wait to talk to them.

Ruthie didn't know what to say. She doubted Moose and Thad did either, but as long as Hucklesford behaved, went to church, and tried to better himself, the three of them had vowed to stand by him. As Moose had said, he had no one else, and it was the right thing to do.

Moose spoke first as he opened the back door to his SUV. "Get in and let's have lunch."

Hucklesford sat in the backseat with Thad while Ruthie sat up front with Moose. Within twenty minutes they drove them to the Burger Stand, a one-story, rambling brick building.

Locals chattered at royal blue booths and wooden tables with chairs with royal blue and pale-yellow swirled cushions. They matched the tablecloths and curtains on the window. The four of them sat at one of the tables. When the waitress arrived, they ordered chili cheeseburgers and French fries.

Ruthie stared at her burger. "The restaurant asked me to rate this entree in a taste test. How'd I do?" She couldn't help but recall the night she and Moose split one in the icy hideout in the backwoods—a dark time before the brightest of days.

"Umm, umm, umm, a humming sound came from Thad's closed mouth, but he pointed at his and gave it a thumbs up."

"It's the best thing I've had since I ate out before I, uh, uh, made the big mistake and ended up in prison."

Ruthie was sorry she'd asked about the burger as tension fell over the table. She tried to think of something to say to make it right, but Moose took care of that.

He held up his entrée. "It's a lot better in this warm restaurant than the leftover sample you brought for us to eat on that cold night in the woods, but hey, that entire episode had a purpose. God brought a lot of good out of the bad." He motioned toward Hucklesford. "What's up next for you?"

Hucklesford sipped his drink, then fiddled with his napkin. "I'm going to work for a detective agency owned by someone Officer Praeger knows." He cut his eyes toward Moose. "I think it's the guy you mentioned, Nick Lancaster."

"Yeah, Nick's a good man, a graduate of Hilltop."

"That's what Officer Praeger said when he scheduled my meeting. Officer Praeger is the biggest reason they made exceptions and gave me this parole." He pulled back his shoulders and held his chin up high. "I finished high school serving time."

Moose and Thad gave him a high-five, and Ruthie clapped. "Congratulations!"

He looked Ruthie in the eye, then Moose and Thad. "I won't let you down. I promise." His voice sounded shaky, as though he didn't know if they approved of him.

He was probably right, because Ruthie didn't know if she approved of him. She'd grasped the unfortunate circumstances in his life. She wanted the best for him and hoped he'd give her a good reason to trust him. Even though it had been two and a half years since she listened to those bullets cracking the ice in that forest, the sound of them still lingered in the back of her brain.

"We're counting on it," Moose said.

"Tell us, man, what can we do for you?" Thad asked.

"Just be my friends. Do ya'll go to church?"

"Yes." A twinge of excitement pricked Ruthie's skin because that was the best place to get acquainted with a new Hucklesford, if there were one. She scooted forward in her seat and leaned across the table. "Please go with us."

"Yeah," Thad chimed in. "I'll introduce you to the college Christian Fellowship." Thad puffed out his chest. "I'm the president. My dad originally insisted I go to UNC, but when he saw how hard I'm working to keep up my grades here, he left well enough alone. That's in his words. I didn't hesitate to get involved in campus life. You know, since I knew I'd be here a while."

"A college group wouldn't accept me, would they?" Hucklesford rubbed the clean, shapely beard on his chin.

Thad sat back in his seat. "Hey man, you need to get a positive outlook. We won't tell them you're on parole. We'll say you're starting a new job, and I invited you to join us as long as you're in the area."

Hucklesford swiped the corner of his eye. "You'd do that for me?"

"Of course I would." Thad pulled a small notepad from his pocket, wrote on the top page, tore it off, and passed it to Hucklesford. "Here's the address. We meet on Sunday nights at seven."

Way to go, Thad. They all needed to support Hucklesford without having him for dinner at their homes, at least until they knew for sure which path he would take. He would need nice clothes to wear to the youth group and on his new job. "Please give me your sizes. I'd like to pick up a few clothing items for you." He could use a jacket, jeans, pants, and a shirt to start, especially if he was going to go to church or hang out with Thad's youth group.

Hucklesford tilted his head and gave Ruthie a confused puppy look. "You don't need to do that."

"I'd like to." She pulled a piece of paper from her purse and passed it to him.

Hucklesford blinked. "All right." He wrote on it and handed it back to her. Taking a deep breath, he relaxed his shoulders. "Someday, I'll pay you back."

"No need. Someday, when you're a successful detective, you'll have an occasion to help someone."

Moose gave Hucklesford a business card. "Call if you need to talk." He leaned back. "Also, I've got an old truck I no longer use. It needs repairs, but my friend owns a garage. I'm sure he'll let us store it there while we use his equipment to fix it up. You can have it."

Hucklesford's mouth flew open. "Really? For real? I could pay you a little at a time."

"We'll see. We may need a handyman occasionally at church. Didn't you handle maintenance at the prison?"

"Yes, I learned how to install sinks, toilets, and showerheads. I can fix leaks too." Hucklesford scooted to the edge of his seat. "That's in addition to the regular stuff, painting, nailing loose boards, most any handyman stuff."

"Sounds good. I think they'll have enough work at the church to pay for the old car in no time."

"Good, because I don't think people would want me in their homes."

Guilt prickled Ruthie's skin. She wouldn't let him in her home until he convinced her he'd turned to Jesus and would obey the law. Obviously, he appeared to want to turn his life around. If he didn't, the prison wouldn't have given him the parole, and Officer Praeger wouldn't have set him up with a job with Nick Lancaster. Hucklesford's mother would be pleased beyond the stars.

"Tell me what's happening with you all. I know Ruthie and Moose are getting married."

Ruthie held up her left hand.

Hucklesford leaned forward and stared at it. "That's beautiful."

Ruthie jerked back her ring. After all, he had robbed a jewelry store. She lowered her chin to her chest. They all had to put Hucklesford's past in the past.

People changed. She no longer wanted a fancy home and a swimming pool. She just wanted Moose.

Hucklesford turned toward Thad. "It sounds like

you're happy at Hilltop College."

Thad nodded. "Yes."

Ruthie finished her burger and sat back. "That was delicious. It looks as though we've all put the bitter cold days and dark nights we spent in these mountains behind us. "If it hadn't been for you…" Ruthie waved toward Hucklesford. "…Moose and I wouldn't have met Thad or each other. Even though Moose and I were at Hilltop College, we existed in worlds apart, with me teaching about nouns and verbs and him coaching athletes to make first downs, block, and tackle. I shudder to think. If our paths had crossed in the hall at the school, we'd neither have lingered nor said more than "Hi.""

Moose moved his hand in a circle. "The four of us share a most unusual bond, but our experience surviving on that freezing, desolate mountain two and a half years ago changed us for the better."

"Ahh, it did," Thad said.

Hucklesford wiped the corners of his eyes.

"God intervened in all our lives and brought good from bad." Ruthie held up her tea, and everyone else did the same. "To the blessings we never imagined when we walked through the storm."

The phrase, "To the blessings," echoed three times before their glasses clinked.

The End.

Did you miss Hidden Danger? You can get it <u>here</u>.

Sign up for Forget Me Not Romances <u>newsletter</u> and receive a special gift compiled from Forget Me Not Authors!

Join our FB pages to keep up on our most current news!

Forget Me Not Romances <u>Readers and Authors</u>

<u>Take Me Away Books</u>

<u>Winged Publications</u>

<u>Soaring Beyond</u>

<u>Fiction and Science Fiction</u>